STUPID CUPID

A NAUGHTY VALENTINE'S MONSTER STUFFER

MAEVE BLACK

STUPID CUPID

A NAUGHTY VALENTINE'S MONSTER STUFFER

MAEVE BLACK

LAUGH
BEST DAY
LOVE YOU
CARE 4 U
SWEET TALK
KISS ME
FRIEND ME
I ♡ YOU

CUPID'S COCKTAIL

1 oz Strawberry Rum
1 oz White Rum
1.5 oz Grenadine
1¼ c Lemon-lime Soda
Top with whipped cream if you're feeling spicy.

TE DE CANELA

Hot Water
Cinnamon Sticks
Sweetener (honey is my go to)

CONTENT WARNINGS

They are detailed on this page so please skip if you don't want spoiler-y stuff.

LAST CHANCE

This takes place before and after Dear Monster Claus. While it's not necessary to read it to enjoy, you'll definitely see many familiar faces and a little sneaky-sneak on who may be coming soon.

There are sexual situations with masochism, honorifics, anal, praise, spitting, D/s dynamics but lite, cinnamon and strawberry cum, a tree trunk shaped dick, punishment (i.e spanking, orgasm denial, and orgasm torture, cockwarming, sex without condoms, slight fire play, frotting, and exhibitionism.

FINAL NOTE

In my worlds, I refrain from all the isms/phobias. This book specifically focuses on two gay men. Queer people can be queer without ridicule or labels. They don't have to explain their style or why they are the way they are.

They're accepted. They're loved. They're never questioned.

They are who they are and no one gets to question that.

<3

love is the whole thing.

we are only pieces.

RUMI

to all those who were
fucked by love
and not in the toe-curling way.

LAUGH

BE DAY

LOVE
YOU

CARE
4 U

SWEET
TALK

KISS
ME

FRIEND
ME

I ♡
YOU

CHAPTER ONE

VALENTINE

Ten Months Before Arson Meets Xo

Stupid Cupid - Mandy Moore

L ove was a delusion both humans and monsters believed in, a sickness that corroded every morsel of their being. And as an anti-love Cupid, I wouldn't be caught dead catching it.

Every single day, I came to work. Yeah, giving love to others had an actual workplace. *Love Hub*. What nonsensical kind of name was that?

My feet were propped on my L-shape desk, rose petals scattered all over, and I just knew it was time for the Valentine's rush.

Every year around the commercial holiday, we had a surplus of charges. One wished for love in their sleep, another went on a dating show, and the worst cases usually existed in best friends who crossed boundaries.

Either way, for the day I was named after, I was booked and bored out of my mind. Grabbing my fizzy drink that I couldn't go a day without, I leaned back in my chair and dazed at the red-and-pink ceiling.

We were everything cliché with the word *love*. Pink and red? Check. Frilly shit and glitter? *Gag*, but check. The most eyesore of decorations on the reg? Also, check.

This place constantly reminded me that love only existed because we made it so. How lame. If people knew our touch created what they held so dear to them, would they even want it? They asked the Fates for affection, romance, and a taste of true love... but we were the creators of that feeling.

It was no wonder they forbade Cupids from finding love, even if they never truly explained why. Sex was on the table, though, something to get us through the fucked-up world of romance. *At least pleasure wasn't fake.* My hand could reference that truth in many ways.

Footsteps clacked toward me, and I immediately knew it was one of my sisters or Paloma—our giver-of-shitty-romance-jobs. They were the only ones who enjoyed evil contraptions on their feet.

"Remember when you asked me if I knew of any... *places*?" she asked randomly, not even saying hello before dropping in. *Ah.* Dulce. Half of the evil twin duo—and my fiend of a sister. Short, adorable, yes, but she packed a brutal punch.

Her hair, much like mine and our two other sisters, was an array of curls. Her nose, with its small stud piercings on both sides, and her ears full of hoops and bars, she was the only sister of mine who stepped outside of the Cupid mold.

"What are you on about?" I questioned my sister, rotating my chair and staring at her peachy eyes. A gleam of mischievousness mirrored there.

"You know," she whispered conspiratorially, waggling her eyebrows. "A *place*." I glanced around the Love Hub, all the Cupids milling about getting work done while my sister planned whatever she was planning.

She let out a low groan when I didn't catch on, but nothing clicked in my brain. Especially not when currently sitting in love hell. Gripping her drink as if it were the only thing keeping her from smacking my head, her hands were white knuckled.

This morning, I received three new charges. Two of them were monsters from Darchon, while one lived in the human realm. The last one, I could at least escape to a few bars and know others would leave me alone. The best part of being coral in color was the avoidance of most humans. While most took the cosplay excuse, others seemed to think I was out of this world.

I was, but it worked as a great repellant either way.

Valentine's was quickly approaching and by quickly, I meant next week. By then, dozens of people would be seeking their forever love.

The grief it gave to follow through consistently exhausted me, but you didn't get the number one spot on the board without my work ethic.

No sleep.

No life.

No happiness.

But no one could compete will my follow-through rate.

I was exactly who I was meant to be. Cupid of all Cupids—*not really,* but really.

"Val!" Dulce complained with a nudge of my shoulder. I finally fixed my gaze on her again. "I've been talking to you for several minutes and you're ignoring me."

"Sorry, D. On deadlines and whatever," I grumbled, not entirely lying. I couldn't stop thinking of how much of an ick romance gave me while also wanting to go get wasted and escape all things love related. Between having a sister who was obsessed with finding love and two others who tortured human guys and monsters alike... I could vacation from the word love forever and it'd be too soon.

She protested, tugging my chair away from my desk, effectively shoving my legs and feet down. With the turn, it forced me to pay attention. Her eyes narrowed as disappointment etched on her forehead. "A month ago, you *begged* me to find out if monsters had sex cl—" I placed a hand over her mouth, frantically eyeing the entire place. Not a single Cupid stared at us. They minded their business, working on their assignments in peace, unlike my sister who nearly shouted my laundry that wasn't dirty whatsoever.

Pain rippled through me as Dulce bit my hand in response. Grumbling, I shook it with pain zinging through. Her lips tilted with amusement, her dimples poking through like she won.

"As I was saying before you rudely interrupted me," she chastised, tapping my head playfully. "I found a play party."

"Like the ones they speak about in the human realm?" I probed, my body flushing at the thought. I'd done a lot of research into humans and kinks. Something about the entire power-exchange dynamic intrigued me.

She nodded enthusiastically, leaning down to whisper in my ear, "I've got you an invite."

"What does that mean?" My throat swelled and dried at the same time, sweat prickling across my skin. I wouldn't know where to start, let alone how to go about joining an event.

"It means they'll reach out to you for rules, attire, and all the finite details. They even have a special mark for newbies. It's a good environment."

"How do you know?" I questioned, my eyebrows skyrocketing on my forehead as doubt lanced through me. Change always held me in a crutch. Between that and my instinct to always run away from what I wanted, people tended to keep their distance.

"Oh, I've been participating," she answered with a smirk. I cringed and waved at her.

"Forget that I asked," I protested, having heard more than I wanted to know about my sister's extracurricular activities. She reached into her pocket, pulling out her cell, typing out something. These phones were much like the ones from the human realm, except we convinced the Ranish fae to make it available off-realm too. Magic got us the best of every world.

"This is all the info you'll need, and you'll be receiving instructions within the next day or so," she clarified while tapping on her phone. "So, little brother, make sure you're at home every day. You don't want to miss their fancy invitation."

My stomach dropped at that, wondering exactly how *fancy* this invite was and if I'd run headfirst into it or away like usual.

As soon as my charges were together, I headed home. Usually, our family lived within the human realm for convenience. Oftentimes, we were only assigned there but on a very rare occasion Darchon called us back.

Two of my three charges were in Darchon—time worked differently there. In Darchon, only moments passed while days, weeks, and sometimes lifetimes passed on Earth. In the case of these two charges of mine, six days passed and tomorrow was Valentine's Day.

Which meant not only was my least favorite day here, but I probably missed my invite to that party Dulce invited me to.

I hated holidays, they were insipid and vain, but I loathed Valentine's Day most. Ironic, since it was my name. Yet, it wasn't *my* day. Instead, people celebrated it by pretending love existed and that they truly cared about the people they bought things for.

I hate it.

Fortunately, that was the only day off in the year that I requested. This year, my wish came true, and they wouldn't be forcing me to work.

My apartment sat in a fairly abandoned area in the human realm. I wasn't even sure what this part of the world was considered, but it didn't get many humans. Chock-full of strawberry fields and beautiful willow trees that made me feel at peace, it seemed free of interruptions.

Xó—my youngest sister—frequently visited, but like me, she dedicated most of her time to her job. Far more than me, in the sense that she believed love was more than the magic we gave others while I stuck to the facts that no one found each other without our help. Not sure where she got the idea that it was an attainable thing, but I tried to encourage her to have hopes, especially since I lost mine long ago.

On my porch rested a black box, not too big, but not too small either.

Exhaustion coated my body as I leaned down, gathering the odd-shaped package. My skin tingled when it connected with the box and I wondered what kind of magic they laced it with.

Sometimes, to be safe from outsiders, monsters would imbue magic warding away humans from areas—or in this case, a package meant for a sex party.

It unfolded as I unlocked my door, twirling in front of me as each piece became one singular box. Ribbon twirled and evaporated before my eyes, and as I set it on my table in the front room, a lone letter, cuff, two masks, and a manila envelope rested.

Picking up the letter, I noted the old Faelic language with a single word. *Aperta.*

My mouth repeated the word, and it opened.

Dear Mr. Amor,

We welcome you to our party. It is masquerade themed, and the only requirement is a mask of your choosing out of the two we've selected for you. Everyone is allowed to feel safe within their designated attire. Whether you like leather, chains, glitter, or less, you're welcome to wear whatever.

We do ask if you plan to be exposed, to hold your wristband and have it bring you directly inside without being seen by outsiders. Human laws may not apply to us in the grander scheme of things, but we like to keep our parties as lawful as possible.

Vex is a monster-only play party venue. It is a dedicated home for events several times throughout the year and we expect our guests to respect the premises so we can continue to host them.

If you're in a committed relationship or partnership, please adhere to collaring dress codes.

If you see someone with a collar, please don't approach them with intentions of playing unless their owners say otherwise. It's always best to ask whenever approaching anyone in any regard to be respectful.

Listed below is every rule for simple play party etiquette, and if you have any more questions with how this gathering will take place, our website linked below will help further your knowledge.

With this being your first time, you'll have a pink wristband; it shows all members that you're new and in need of patience and practice.

We're very excited to meet you. Please fill out this questionnaire that details every kink known to man and monster alike. It'll be given to the host before your arrival, and will help us magically mark your wristband with what you seek. See you soon.

Sincerely,

Amadis

Senior Coordinator

My fingers shook as I held the invitation. Part of me hoped I'd missed the package, knowing that receiving it meant giving in to what I avoided for so long. Setting it down next to the manila envelope, I gripped it and went over the detailed kinks.

With every new one not known to me, my eyes widened. There was one listed for flames. Flames, like *fire*. Fire, like *dragon*. My chest hammered, sweat lining my forehead. Dragons were nonexistent in Darchon, they had been gone for centuries, and the thought of seeing one brought an intense kind of excitement through me.

Watersports, bondage, cream pies, and so many more were listed and I made sure to research every single one.

Sure, some weren't my cuppa, but I just moved along as I went through them. The ones that caught my attention and held it while watching videos were orgasm denial and orgasm torture. My chest tightened just from reading those four words as my heartbeat seemed to skyrocket simultaneously. Clamminess met my palms, and I knew the visceral reaction to the videos turned me on.

Yeah, something about both intrigued every part of me.

I wasn't a virgin, nor was I new to pleasure. Yet, no matter what experiences occurred in the past, nothing kept my attention, and it never went on for more than one round with my one-night partners.

But this... *kink*, it finally clicked in my brain. I wanted this, my body felt it too. As soon as I finished marking the possible interests, I signed my name and it vanished into thin air.

Well, okay then.

For the next two hours, I made sure to go over every detail he listed. What to wear, what to do if you wanted to ask a Dom to play. How to respect boundaries and ask for consent in every situation. If a scene happened in the Viewing Room, it was where everyone could watch, but there were still rules there too.

If people were fucking in a hallway, unless they asked for you to join, it would be best to continue walking.

And if you planned on joining a scene, or were invited, under no circumstance were you allowed to use meinshine, or any other incapacitating drink, inhalant, or edible.

Even if liquid courage intrigued me, breaking that rule was an immediate removal from the premises. They took it very seriously.

I flipped through the pages on asking a Dom for play. My stomach fluttered as my eyes danced over the words.

Each one was different. Some might request you to kneel, some want silence and your neck bared to them, and others might want to have a conversation before they even considered you, but most important was simply getting consent and proceeding from there.

My nerves settled a little at the realization these parties seemed very laid-back and structured at the same time, even if people were involved in live scenes. I wanted to smack myself for having such stigmatized and vanilla concepts on how these events worked.

Something clicked for me as I finished perusing the FAQs on their website, and I knew, this was where I was meant to escape.

Maybe for the first time ever, I wouldn't be entirely miserable on Valentine's Day.

CHAPTER TWO

PYRO

Take On Me - a-ha

Restless.

For as long as I'd been an adult, my limbs grew heavier, achy, like there was something missing that I couldn't quite put my finger on.

When I worked, fulfilling my duties as Arson's babysitter, the feeling festered, crawling over my skin like spiders seeking refuge.

I always knew I'd become Santa someday, it was all I ever known and planned for. My only goal in life revolved around that fact.

Rarely did I live, go out, have sex, or enjoy the simple things immortal life offered. Even when I went to sex clubs and play parties at private events, spent nights with men and monsters alike, I didn't truly give in to the temptation to make love a permanent fixture in my life.

When one took the Santana vow, it was a free life. No children, no commitments outside of work, and definitely no split attention. Not unless you didn't want to be the man in the red suit.

Being Santa required every single day of your life. From day one to three-sixty-five, I worked tirelessly. Even being the middle-ish child, I still did the most. Arson hated his position and as the mature brother, I kept him on track for the sake of our family legacy.

Like me, he wanted more, yet he would stay Santa long before I ever got the chance. He never took the job seriously, though. Unless he found someone worth loving, I didn't see myself becoming Santa for at least another century or two. We were close in age, and that probably related to this inane need to slow my own life down along with his own.

It was Valentine's. This last Christmas being a shit show of all proportions meant there was only ten months to get our shit together for this year. Arson dragged his feet, his lack of care for this once in a lifetime opportunity twisted in my gut like a knife lodged deep, hitting every vital organ on the way out.

If not for me, the last five Christmases wouldn't have happened, either. Yet, you didn't hear him giving me thanks for my efforts.

My body buzzed as anger and discomfort touched me. We were lovers, anger and I. Control was never a hard thing for me, but resentment grew deep, a wound that never quite healed. It was a hardened scar, reopening with every disappointment, begging me to stop digging at it.

It led me to Vex tonight, to escape, and it'd been years since I decided to go. Too many disappointments in my day led me to spiral. Whether that be drinking or insomnia, neither were a healthy outlet and at the least, releasing within a scene might be a safer bet.

To no avail, Vex themself always invited me. Every event, even though I hadn't been to one in years, they sent an invite in hopes of pulling me from retirement. I respected that, the loyalty and commitment. My life lacked that sort of consistency.

A black box resided on my desk, stacked on top of the heaps of letters, drawings, and other misshapen items people delivered out of love for Santa. My hands hovered over the box, visually tracing the outline of it. I already knew what exist inside, but I couldn't bring myself to quite commit.

Unlike most monsters my age, I lived at the North Pole. A constant babysitter for my brother, making sure he handled everything, while my life passed me.

Fun was a rare thing in my life, and when it was within my grasp, Arson interrupted. Unintentionally, of course, but I'd always been the fixer.

Couldn't get something done, *call Pyro.*

Wanted to fuck around, *text Pyro.*

Needed reprieve to complain, *Pyro had nothing better to do.*

Not tonight.

The package surged through me when I finally lifted it. Vex always enchanted them, making sure only the intended recipient could see the contents inside.

Without needing to unravel it, the ribbon split and disappeared as it unveiled the letter, wristband, and a mask.

The letter fluttered open and the grin couldn't escape my face if it tried.

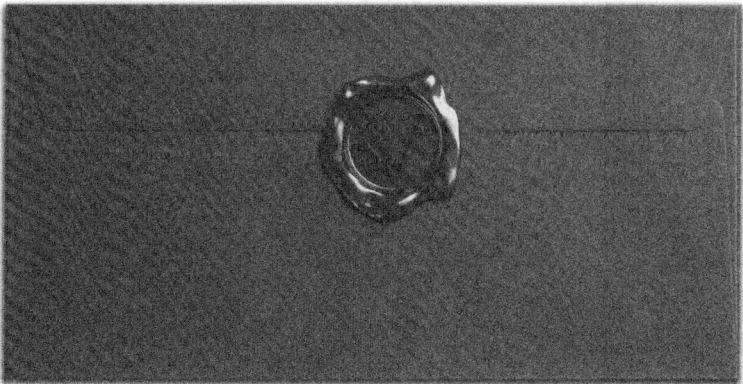

Dearest Pyro,

It's been ages, old friend. I know you're out there being the next Aita, focusing on what matters. But as usual, I have an invite. There will be fresh meat, and one in particular filled out his questionnaire with some things I know you'd be intrigued with. If you're up for joining, you know where to send your RSVP. And of course, wear the mask, masquerade themed. Since you're a tight ass and always wear suits, I don't see this being an issue for you. Starts tonight at eight. Be early, you know you like to feel around first anyway.

With love and insult,

Vex

I chuckled with mirth, missing the old bat. Vex was an ancient-as-all hell *Saephyn,* they were fae who required blood consumption to survive, much like vampires in human myths. We'd been friends for so long, life seemed to exist along with our friendship.

The navy mask they gave me fit my face like a glove. As I pressed it to my eyes, it felt magically inclined to adapt to me.

That monster was smart.

I didn't truly want to come out tonight. For years, I avoided events, knowing I couldn't get attached. It wasn't easy to jump into a scene without getting to know my partner first. Sure, experiencing one-night commitments where they were at my mercy appealed to a singular part of me, but I also wanted them comfortable and partners were more pliant and free where time wasn't an issue. That way the awkward stage passed with the negotiation stage and not rushed for a quick power exchange that left me hankering for more.

There was a lot to being a part of this world. The most important things were being safe, sane, and consensual. Which made this specific party so enticing, everyone was here for their own reason. Vex vetted every single person who entered their domain. Everyone made mistakes and no one was a true expert, but everyone here knew what to expect and accidents hardly happened.

Even monsters had needs, and this event—much like the rest—was safe for us to experience our desires freely. Especially when your craving was exhibitionism and voyeurism. Things that often could get you arrested in the human realm. Other monster things were illegal in most other realms too, and being in an environment like Vex's kept them safe.

My body tightened with nerves as I grasped the cuff adorned to my wrist. Much like a watch, it sat perfectly without bothering me. Within moments, it flashed me to the location of one of Vex's places. He had many, and some were in pockets, magically infused places that didn't exist in any realm, but instead, floated in an abyss.

Tonight, I'd be playing. Knowing what I wanted was easy, I cultivated my tastes over eons, carving out each and every one with what felt good and what didn't do it for me. Vex telling me they had someone in mind helped eased most of my tension. Maybe he wanted someone to help him let go.

Someone like... me.

Filled with many monsters tonight, the options were endless. Each one who arrived here were labeled—but not by our species. Instead, we were labeled by our status. Whether new, seasoned, or in between. An added layer of labeling further detailed if attendees were taken, wanting submissives, or seeking play partners. Mine showed my single status, and that I sought a playmate.

My eyes connected with familiar old ones. Red, glazed with promise, and waiting, he sauntered toward me.

I took several steps toward him, noting the pet at his feet on their hands and knees with a collar. They were adorable, sporting a muzzle studded with red jewels. My eyes met my old friend's once more.

"Pyro," he rasped, his monstrous voice something that took me years to get used to. Bruno was an *Anguis*, a basilisk. His vocal cords always carried a slither of sorts, like he tasted every word as it came out. "This is Rico, my pet."

Rico didn't glance up, but rubbed their face against Bruno's leg. He tapped their head in praise, giving me a knowing smirk.

"You're alone," he noted, his hands tracing the empty space around me. I nodded, not needing to explain what he already knew. My reputation in the community revolved around my future and my boundaries resulting from those choices. Bruno directed his head toward the other room. "It's been a while."

"Busy," I answered, thinking of how my life changed since my last visit to one of these parties. Arson's declining desire to be Santa and how it altered every choice down to not leaving home much. Not even for drinks and friendship.

When you were immortal, time didn't seem to be such a big deal, but I tracked it consistently, watching as it ticked by without me existing in it.

"Brother in trouble?" His eyebrow raised, as if he knew how deep the dread went. Bruno and I went way back. We met at a party not too different than this one. He knew I wasn't the oldest but burdened with the responsibilities all the same.

"Not in trouble, no," I answered, thinking of Arson. We'd always been close. My brother tended to take the family business less seriously than any other Santana. Maybe my work ethic was better than his, but he seemed inclined to avoid his duties as much as possible.

"He seems to be pursuing something other than his destiny."

"Destiny seems so on the nose, no?" Bruno questioned, placing a hand on his pet. He stroked them, his fingers coiling into their black curls. "He doesn't want to be Santa?"

I shook my head. "Not anymore, and it's getting increasingly difficult to get him to take charge of his responsibilities," I admitted, scratching my chin. Anxiety burrowed itself deep within my chest, knowing that letting this out would create a slight ease of tension, even if only temporary. "It's exhausting to be the parent to him when he's older."

Bruno nodded thoughtfully, walking toward the private room with chaise lounges and other furniture. "I think you should take a playmate," he conceded, sitting on the leather chair and pointing at his feet for his pet to settle. Immediately, they did, curving between his legs and rubbing their face all over. It was endearing, seeing the dedication in their eyes as they nuzzled Bruno with affection. "Even if only temporarily."

"I haven't taken a playmate in ages," I confessed, my palms sweating at the risk of falling for someone, coming to care for their well-being and losing my chance to ever become Santa. "I can't do long term." Yet, I couldn't be strictly platonic. My heart easily cared for others.

"Then make it an agreement, with all the usual negotiations but add that in there. Be up front and they'll choose based off of that."

The fact that the answer was so simple had my eye twitching. Why did I ever overthink this? Bruno was right. Honesty was something I valued above all else, being true with a partner was the least I could do.

Would they want that? No strings attached playtime? Where we could meet and *not* catch feelings? Would they accept my proposition?

My chest warmed at the prospect, nestling hope underneath my rib cage, tapping against my sternum where I hid the rest of my hopes and dreams.

"I'll do it," I breathed out, relief flooding my veins. This admission alone was something *I* needed, and maybe the playmate would seek simplicity too.

I bid Bruno farewell a while later, and headed toward the comingling area. Each room designated for everything you could think of. Upstairs, there were rooms for quiet and private play, where prying eyes were forbidden.

They had a specified area for everything. Watersports and other fluid-sharing kinks were near the end of the hall, labeled with specifications.

Also near there on the right side were rooms designated for other play that wasn't something I ever really ventured into and some I'd never heard of.

In the main area, they called it the Viewing Room, was where voyeurism, exhibitionism, and sharing took place. If you were there, you actively sought for one of those—especially to be watched by others.

There was, of course, another area where you could find playmates that was more private. Depending on my mood, I might take that area instead.

If you want privacy after choosing a mate in the Viewing Room, you could also take it upstairs, but it was the free space where everyone kind of mingled and played out together where the majority of monsters hung out.

Always ask for consent first. Always. Even in the Viewing Room.

A red monster with massive horns straddled another in the center, slowly gyrating up and down. Their size difference was magnificent, and I wondered if my partner would be smaller than me.

My eyes immediately caught on their muscular forms. Similar to mine but different all the same. The one on the ground was covered in leather. Their body a simple tool for others' usage. The one above, using the one beneath, took their pleasure. The sounds of whimpering had my dick twitching with promise.

Voyeurism triggered a hedonistic part of me. Where I wanted people to watch me bring my partner to orgasm over and over, and knew that *I* put them in that position of convulsing release. It soothed a primal part of me. One that sated the beast within who constantly begged to be uncaged.

Taking a chair in the corner of the Viewing Room, surrounded by books, felt on par with my personality. It comforted me to be encircled by literature, even if twenty feet away monsters fucked vigorously.

Let the fun begin.

LAUGH
BEST DAY
LOVE YOU
CARE 4 U
SWEET TALK
KISS ME
FRIEND ME
I ♥ YOU

CHAPTER THREE

VALENTINE

All My Life - K-Ci & JoJo

"**W**elcome," a person greeted as soon as I strolled through the door. They were in a mask, much like mine, corresponding to the theme.

I thought it a little cliché to have masks here. Trust and honesty being a requirement to entering, after all. Something about others hiding put me on edge, which should be funny since I hid most days. Trust issues swam through my veins, but tonight, I'd willingly give that up.

Since my invite last night, I researched what it meant to join a play party. The rules, the etiquette, and things to be respectful of. They said you always made mistakes your first few times, and a part of me hoped to escape that embarrassment.

"Name?" the person requested, twirling a pen between their fingers. Their eyes met mine with enthusiasm. Amethyst, soft, and colorful at the same time. Maybe being cautious was an overreaction on my part and this would be an amazing first experience.

Let go.

I needed to.

Taking a massive breath, I let it out steadily. "Valentine Amor," I answered. Their painted nails tapped over the stack of papers before nodding knowingly. They whispered a few words and a bright pink glitter wristband of sorts appeared next to my other one.

Witnessing Cupid magic took my breath away at times, but it was simpler. A little dazzling gleam and then love happened. But this? A next-level type of experience seeing something appear out of nowhere. It was physical and tangible.

"What is that for?" I asked, gripping my hands nervously. Their eyebrows hiked up a little, amusement there.

"It tells them you're single and searching for a Dominant or top." *Top*. My body tingled at the word. Not once fooling around with random monsters did I let someone inside me. Part of me craved it, but giving that kind of power to someone hadn't been on my radar until I ventured into the scene.

I swallowed, the dryness of my throat leaving me parched. With a nod, I adjusted my leather vest. The attire was listed as comfortable. So I picked the black mask to match my studded jacket, knowing that underneath it, I was still me.

Making my way through the place, I noted visible signs designating each area. After reading the FAQ, I knew that the direction I headed contained open scenes and people who might want a partner.

Nerves coiled beneath my skin as my steps drew me nearer. This place reminded me of old Victorian buildings. Gothic and dense, with vintage armoires and chaises. As I entered the designated Viewing Room, my skin flamed. There were monsters in many different stages of undress. Several were gathered in the center, spanking people with crops, and face sitting as well. There was even a trio linked together, rutting ruthlessly, while others gathered to watch.

I didn't linger on them for too long, not wanting to stay in one place. There was a slight urgency inside me, begging me to find someone who caught my attention and captivated me enough to erase my nerves.

The room was massive, mostly empty of the vintage pieces the other areas had. However, it did have a lot of chairs, tables, and other leather-bound objects for use. I couldn't keep up with all of them as I made my way through.

No one paid me any attention, my eyes not connecting with anyone's as I trailed the room like a lost puppy.

In the corner, near a wall full of books, sat a monster—no, a dragon. *I think.* Wings wide and expanding around him like a threat, my body tingled. Fire play now made perfect sense.

A pinch inside my stomach tapped against me, a flush building under my skin. Whether that feeling resulted from attraction or some weird desperation, I didn't know, but the desire to crawl and approach him nearly had me falling to my knees.

My body throbbed at the prospect of being at his mercy, giving in to him and submitting. Unlike most of the attendees I noticed, he wore a suit. From head to toe, he seemed the image of a strict monster. His navy-blue button-up fit his body, matching his skin almost entirely, while his vest over it only accentuated the fact that he was massive.

His thighs were thick, muscular, and his slacks cupped him like a hug, something I also wanted to do. All my reactions shocked me. Not once had it occurred to me that I'd crave full submission.

My thoughts ran wild with imagery. Of him holding me down, drilling into me, all while he told me how good I was.

A full-body shudder went through me as I hesitantly approached him. Did he want me to kneel? I'd drop to my fucking knees just to have his attention only on me. *What is with this reaction to a stranger?*

The moment his eyes hit my own, my legs trembled. What the fuck? The instinctual way my body craved to fall hit me stronger than any experience prior.

His gaze screamed intrigue and demand, a dance of power and giving I didn't quite understand. Did I say something first? *Did he?*

Heat gathered across my arms and bare chest, my nipples hardening as lewd ideas filled me. Never in my life had someone brought this kind of reaction from me. Sure, attraction existed for me, even strict lust for fucking came and went on occasion. But this? It was pure subservience fueling me to him. My feet didn't stop, but fuck, they should.

Rushing into something went against every morsel of my being. Slow and sure was my usual approach, it kept me safe and in control.

He languidly separated his thighs, easing into a relaxed sitting position. Then, he tapped his spread legs, the air of confidence unraveling my sense of restraint. "Sit, pet," he directed. My gaze fell to his lap, the sure way he sat with poise. Part of me stalled, the insolent part that rebelled at any type of demand. It was the exact reason I wanted to relinquish control. It would ease me into a trust, help me learn to give in where it mattered.

When my knees didn't immediately buckle, against all signs of my yearning, his narrowed gaze reached my nervous one. "Ah, you must be new." His eyes flickered to my labeled wristbands. A sharp nod was my only offer, my spine tingling with the need to beg for forgiveness. "When my pets misbehave, they get reprimanded."

I gulped, my body overheating with his stare alone. "I'm sorry," I blurted out, immediately shuddering at his single raised eyebrow.

"Sorry would be you sitting on my lap, remedying your mistake," he explained, watching me closely. An exhale left me quickly. More of a huff mixed with the brattiness settling inside me. When I didn't immediately move, he chuckled darkly. His eyes flashing with a type of reproach that should scare me far more than it should excite me.

My cheeks warmed as I pictured the others behind me somewhere, doling out beatings. Would he do the same to me?

"Some don't take impoliteness as a good thing," he mused, again tapping his thigh. "Since you're fresh, I'll give you a choice. Either you sit on my lap and ask what I know is burning on the tip of that tongue of yours, or you walk away. My time is precious, and I have rules. If you want to know them and how I admonish my pets for disobedience, sit."

Fear registered, stopping all fight within me, and I sat my ass down on his thigh. As if it weren't enough, he rotated me closer to his chest, bringing us flush.

Leaning into my ear, his hot breath sent shivers down my spine. "Good boy," he praised, and my entire body lit up at the simple words. "Ah, you like that." He stroked my jaw with a look of interest flaring in his eyes. "Now, proceed."

I trembled as his one palm traced the skull pattern on the back of my vest. Sitting here immediately felt comforting. Relaxing almost. He wasn't overly hulking in comparison to me, but he definitely had a lot more muscle than my lean frame.

"I've never done this before," I admitted on an exhale. He didn't interrupt me or ask anything, rubbing circles on my lower back, expectant. "But I want to be—topped." The way my voiced dropped by the end had amusement reflecting in his eyes.

They were green, viciously green, like muddled seaweed.

"Would you like to continue this in private, or was one of your interests being watched by others?" His voice was stoic, no inflection in his tone, and it allowed me to clearly think without knowing what he preferred.

Part of me didn't mind the thought of him touching me where others could wish I was them, but the bigger part of me that never experienced this wanted privacy. At least for this time.

"Private," I murmured, my blood rushing through me. It was as if I could feel each pump of my heart, every beat as it echoed in my ears.

"Very well," he replied, standing and bringing me with him. The ease in which he held me comforted me on a deep level.

He carried me all the way up the staircase, his head tipping toward a person in all purple. The visual exchange of them had me curious, but no words were uttered as we passed. By the time we made it upstairs, my body melded to his with ease. There wasn't anything quite like being held.

Sitting, with me still in his embrace, I exhaled a contented sigh.

"What's your name, pet?" My eyes blinked lazily at him, wondering how effortlessly I fell into this. He waited only a moment more before giving my ass a small pinch.

I nearly bounced off his thigh. "Valentine," I expressed, noting how he mentally seemed to trace the word. "Yours?"

"Pyro. When we're doing this, you can call me anything that comforts you." *I liked that I got to choose.*

"You're cute and coral, are you an incubus?"

Immediately, heat hit my face as I realized it wouldn't be too off the mark. While Cupids didn't require sex energy, we were of fae origin.

"Cupid."

His eyes widened a smidgen, a little tilt of his lips displayed before he leaned into my ear. "Cupid is real?" he questioned, a bit of awe to his tone.

"Cupids," I corrected. "Yes, we're love givers." As if entranced with me, his eyes met my lips. The instant intimacy had me wiggling. "And are you..." I paused, thinking of how his wings expanded behind us. "A dragon?"

A little rumble traced my spine. "Yes, pet. Does that excite you?"

"Yes," I admitted, thinking of touching them—licking them, even.

"Good. I like when my pet is happy." *Pet.* Singular, as in only me. Relief had me exhaling a sigh. Weirdly enough, I didn't think being with someone who planned on being with others tonight was in the cards for me.

"How does this work?" I asked, turning my face to his. Our lips were mere centimeters away from each other's, and I shook, losing focus from our close proximity once more.

"We discuss negotiations, and go from there."

I nod, accepting this with silence.

"I have three rules that can't be broken," he started, tracing my back once more. "First, no lying. You must be honest with me. Don't hold back. Without communication, we can't proceed safely. Whether that's something as simple as responding to a question I've asked or as detrimental as you hiding pain. We must be open."

I let out a little noise, and I hoped he hadn't heard it, but immediately, he gripped my jaw, the warmth from his fingers mixed with the heat from his eyes dragged a gasp from me.

"Is honesty hard for you, Valentine?" Him saying my name so demandingly elicited an immediate reaction. Shit. This connection felt too real, too fast.

I offered a nod. "I've always struggled with being open, emotions, and letting go." His eyes narrowed but something must've clicked for him because he continued with his rules.

"Second, I require you to be mine and only mine while we're together." As if he knew I felt the same, his gaze softened and he leaned forward. "Thirdly, I want you on time. Don't be late. Be naked and ready for me unless otherwise instructed. If you're late, I will punish you."

"Understood."

"Now, tell me what you like," he requested, his face still hovering close. It was hard to concentrate when all I wanted to do was touch his skin and feel how warm it was.

"I don't share well," I admit, swallowing the dryness from my mouth. "I'm not into a ton of masochism, but impact and fire play..." I sucked in a breath as flames danced in his eyes. "That intrigues me."

"Go on," he encouraged.

"I've never been topped. Until recently, I never wanted to."

"What changed your mind?" His hand rested on my lower back, a silent support that no one had ever gotten close enough to me to offer.

"Until finding monster porn, I didn't feel interested."

His face didn't change, but somehow, I knew he wanted me to give more details. "I hooked up with a lot of humans who were privy to our kind and some monsters, but I always topped. It felt good, but it also didn't satisfy me. Something always felt wrong, like I was missing an intrinsic part."

He nodded, his thumb rubbing up and down my spine, lulling me into a sense of comfort. "My sister told me that monster porn was a thing, and I fell into a hole. *Not like that,*" I immediately corrected. An amused curl of his lips was my only response. "There were legitimate ones for D/s relationships, and being topped but with power exchange, and I realized it was what I was missing."

"You're being so open with me, pet, I'm so proud of you." His words caused a stir in my jeans. A pulsing throb straight to my dick. My physical reaction to his words only reaffirmed my need for praise within this arrangement.

"I enjoy that," I confessed. His hand stilled and he turned my chin toward him.

"Praise brings pleasure, noted," he responded, that little lip tilt the only expression allowing me to know he approved. "When you're good, I'll reward you handsomely." His thumb traced my bottom lip, touching the metal rings on both sides. Our eyes connected with reciprocated lust at the action. "But if you're bad, and break my rules, I will punish you."

A jolt raced through me, but not with fear or apprehension—thrill. "I don't know if they'll be good for me."

He shook his head immediately. "Punishment isn't entirely meant to feel good, but not all pain is unpleasant," he expressed, his other hand still tracing my back. "Some find pleasure in their pain, but what punishment is meant to do is give enforcement, and I positively reinforce it with rewards. You should want to please me when I've earned that part of you. As I will want to please you too."

My body strained with arousal, achiness my only companion. "I think that's all I can think of," I admitted, keeping my hands to myself.

"Well, let me tell you my hopes. I hope that we enjoy our time together, and you fall apart for me. I want to undress you and mark you for others to know that while we do this, you're mine. We can meet up once every other week, unwind, and keep it to play only. After every scene, I'd like for us to discuss what you liked and disliked, and before, what your preferred aftercare looks like. While I want to create a good time for us both, I can't get emotionally attached in the sense of relationships. So, I'd prefer we keep it sexual in nature."

I gulped, knowing that was exactly what I came here for but realizing hearing it from him saddened me. A small part of me hoped for a friendship out of this.

"Is friendship off the table?" The words left me in a rush before I could rein them back in. He stated a boundary of no comingling outside of our scenes and already, I overstepped.

His sucked in a breath but beneath the caution, his eyes flashed with interest. "Friendship is acceptable." Relief filled me. And I didn't understand why the fuck I cared.

CHAPTER FOUR

PYRO

These Arms of Mine - Otis Redding

"What do you want from this?" From the moment we met, hesitation stopped his lips from moving, but that was the first habit he needed to break.

My eyes trailed his cheeks, flushed from my question, and he seemed to be sweating like he couldn't breathe. He sat on my lap and it took everything in me to hide my arousal.

No response.

He knew the rules, I put them on the table only minutes ago, explaining my expectations, as he did his. Eyes met mine, coral, a red that bordered on a dark side of a poppy. As he watched me, it reminded me of a pleased pet. He enjoyed being on my lap, craved my touch, and the way praise lit him up brought me so much peace. Yet, he already fought me. Soon, he'd ease from that immediate distrust.

"Words, Valentine," I instructed, my body flushing with purpose. There was no way to truly describe what it felt like to have a submissive on their knees, begging for something but unable to ask. The difference with them on your lap, looking at you as if you held the world in your palms... priceless.

He'd learn to obey.

I'd teach him.

A deep inhale dragged me closer, needing to touch him more somehow, to know what felt good to him and why he seemed so guarded.

"Remember the rules?" I prodded, and his eyes fell to the floor, the way his shoulders tightened gave him away. "What's the first and most important?"

"Be honest."

I nodded but reached forward, tipping his chin with my fingers. His eyes glossed over, affection and nerves dancing there. "Why do you avoid telling the truth now?" He shook his head with a smidgen of defiance. Straightening his spine, he let out a deep breath.

"This is hard for me," he admitted, his body tense and wound tight. I wanted to unravel him, show him that giving in would lessen his stress, and free him of the confines he strangled himself in. "I've never been one to open up about my life."

"I don't need your life, pet. I need your freedom."

Our eyes connected once more, a soft peace settling there. Acceptance. He nodded. "It's yours."

His body quaked as we stared eye to eye. I never considered myself a hard Dom, just a pleasure control top with soft Dom tendencies. Someone who liked control but through their partner's pleasure while also controlling the way it happened. I wanted him to feel good. Even if he'd learn to feel it through the littlest of pain.

"What's your safe word?" My guided words had his eyes glimmering with desire. His teeth snagged on his lip, brushing his piercings with malice.

"Red. Yellow to slow down."

"Good," I praised. "It's time for your punishment now." His eyes dilated, his body shaking. Whether that reflected his fear or bliss, I didn't know yet.

"But I—"

"Never answered me," I gentle scolded, interrupting his excuse. "You also disobeyed my number one rule. By not answering, you're being dishonest. We have to be open. Honesty is important to have a good time together. How can I take care of you when you don't tell me what's affecting you?"

He let out a little grumble, drawing a little growl out of me. His face cleared of pouting immediately, then he nodded once more.

I stood, letting him stand alone as I made my way to the leather chaise lounge. It was black, smooth, with the most delicate sewing patterns. Sitting there, I waggled my finger at him.

"Undress."

Apprehension flickered across his face, but he removed his vest anyway. Next, he took off his boots, socks, and went for his jeans. I didn't allow him an ounce of privacy. Instead, I sat comfortably, spreading my legs, and rested my elbows on my thighs. The appearance of disinterest I portrayed had a flush creeping over him.

Once his clothes were removed, I studied him. Intrigue and arousal swam together in my abdomen. My cock twitched, wanting to be fisted and soothed, but tonight was about him. Tonight, his pleasure would be mine.

"On my lap, face down," I directed, my body heating at the sensation of his curiosity. While he'd undressed before coming toward me, I stayed in my clothing. This was about him—his punishment—he'd have to earn seeing me in a state of undress.

His feet dragged as he made his way over, his body blushing beautifully. From head to toe, tattoos covered him. Some were in old Faelic, words many have forgotten. Some were serpents, tracing his muscles as if coiled to do so. There was a specific one that drew my attention over the other. An anatomical heart squeezed by a boney fist. The pain depicted stirred a sense of concern I shouldn't have.

Something else definitive caught my eye too. His cock. Not once had I ever considered one beautiful, but Valentine's was nice and thick, veins straining on the underside. Along with those were six barbels that triggered a feral part of me.

I wanted to lick him from root to tip, see how long I could prolong his pleasure until he cried for me to stop.

I craved that more than my next breath of air, but it would have to wait. Doling out his punishment came first, and knowing his fear of letting himself be honest would be something to break him of.

Part of being in this kind of agreement meant communication and comfortability. I wanted to take care of him, be what he needed, and in return, I only sought his truths.

MAEVE BLACK

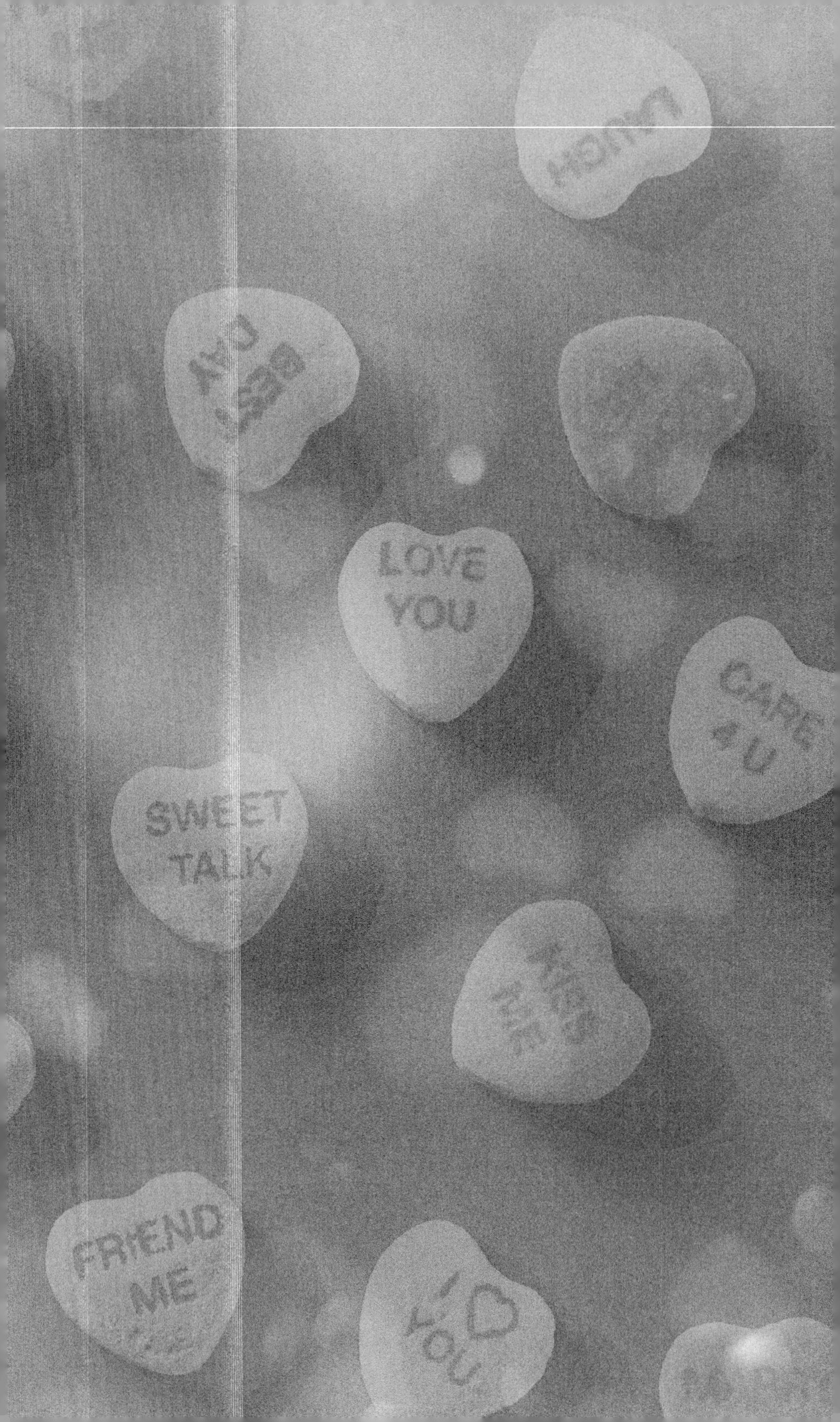
LAUGH
BEST DAY
LOVE YOU
CARE 4 U
SWEET TALK
FRIEND ME

CHAPTER FIVE

VALENTINE

All of Me - John Legend

He was going to spank me. Not even fifteen minutes passed where he told me he hated dishonesty. It was a hard limit for him. The thought never occurred to me, that people would hate lying so much.

I lived most of my life in mistruths to protect myself.

Whether it was something little about liking someone or wanting more from them.

This was my scariest truth, being touched intimately. I wanted to bathe in his arms and allow him to hold me while I just existed in his warmth. Sitting in his lap only reaffirmed my denial.

The thoughts confused me, brought on a fear of all new levels. I wasn't affectionate. My family never did that, and neither did I.

My friends gave side hugs and compliments, but the deeper part of that never was given to me.

"In the future, when I ask a question, I expect an answer," he clarified, tapping his thick thighs for me to be on his lap.

The moment I saw him in the Viewing Room, his wings pressing outward like a warning, and my body reacted. My feet took me toward him before my brain could tell me to stop.

Call it fate or even attraction, but I saw his eyes as I drew nearer, the depthless green almost serpentine and slithering. They commanded me without words and it had me near kneeling.

While waiting for my invitation, I studied play party etiquette and didn't realize how real the draw of people could be.

I felt safe here. Scared from the newness of my environment, but safe all the same. If not for their website detailing all the rules, I might've not felt so inclined. His eyes hadn't left mine since noticing me in the room. They scoured my body, the leather vest, my tattoos, and while his body seemed entirely unaffected, his eyes told me everything I needed to know.

"Valentine," he rasped, drawing me back to the room. He raised an eyebrow. "This can't work if you're not present."

I nodded. "I was thinking of the moment I noticed you," I admitted, knowing I had to give him something. Anything to keep him here. If he left from me breaking the rules, I'd fall apart. Whether or not he realized it yet, I needed this.

He had as much decision in this as I did. Both of us could walk away, never see each other again. That thought alone had fear sluicing through me like a deadly poison.

"Bend," he directed. I did, laying across him and the couch. It felt smooth beneath my skin and he felt hard. The contrast drew a contented sigh from me. "Continue."

"I thought about the moment of being in your presence," I told him, my blood humming with arousal. It was potent being this vulnerable for someone you didn't know. Giving them trust and having the expectation of them handling it with care. "You sat there with such nonchalant dominance." His hand smoothed across my ass, his touch warm and inviting. It didn't occur to me that being touch starved meant every caress would ignite my skin.

"Six hits is your punishment. If you behave, I'll give you a reward after," he explained. "Count for me, pet." Without warning, his hand was bearing down on my right cheek, the resulting sting brought a throbbing pulse in my dick. Shit.

"One," I hissed, not knowing if the pain was entirely discomfort or if pleasure drove my reaction. His palm came down over my left cheek then, this time harder. My skin flamed with heat, and a moan ripped from me before I could hold it in. "Two."

His hand soothed the burn, kneading my cheeks with care. "You're doing so well for me," he commended, and my entire body blazed. I learned new things about this monster with every interaction. "Keep talking," Pyro encouraged, his hands still moving across my bare skin.

"You stole my thoughts and erased my caution, I wanted to kneel for you in the doorway and crawl your way," I confessed, my face hot as hell with shame. Did I just say that?

His hand came down quickly and I yelped with the strength of the hit. Tears stung my eyes and I sucked in the pain. My dick didn't get the discomfort memo because it leaked, and I was certain he knew, or at the very least, he felt it. "Three." It came out as a whimper and then he swatted again. "Four."

Tears trickled from my eyes as the pain and pleasure danced together, my balls aching for something and I wasn't sure what that was. With my dick pressed upward, it felt suffocated and tight. Torment wound inside my stomach, twisting like a spiral readying to destroy everything in its path. My release was moments away, and he hadn't yet touched me.

"Last two," he rasped, his voice affected and heady with lust.

As I adjusted, bracing myself for the pain, I wiggled and felt something massive and hard against me. *Fuck*. He could be stiff and stoic with expressions and mostly even tones but he liked this too, his erection reassured me this wasn't merely one-sided.

His hand slapped against my lower cheek on my left and then my right side, a new string of curses flew past my lips as pain bit at me.

My body shook with adrenaline and desire, something I'd never experienced on this level.

"Shit," I whimpered, my body overheating with need. "Five and six," I hurried to remedy with my words.

He lifted me easily, this man so fucking strong that shock escaped my lips. "So good for me, pet," he applauded and I lit up, his eyes dancing over my face. "You took your punishment with ease." My entire body coiled for release. If he so much as kissed me right now, I'd fall apart.

Kiss?

My mind stumbled on that thought. I couldn't kiss him. Kissing him meant feelings, and feelings were off-limits. Why did my mind immediately travel with that desire in mind?

I shook off the longing to do exactly that and sucked in a shaky breath. His eyes scanned me, care and concern twisting across his features, and my stomach burned with an ache I couldn't describe.

"Now for your reward," he purred, his eyes darkening as he smirked. It was the first facial expression that entirely overtook his face, morphing it.

I thought he was handsome prior to when all he offered was stiffness and calm, but that tilt of his lips, and the way he devoured me with that one look, undid me.

"Please," I asked, not knowing why I was begging him. As if my response was exactly what he sought, he nipped my throat and stood with me in his arms. "On the bed."

His demand was soft and playful, something that didn't exist five minutes ago. My ass stung as the air hit it. It reminded me that this may be a reward, but I still fucked up by not being honest with him.

"On your back," he directed as I began to crawl across it. "You never finished telling me how you wanted to crawl." Humor laced his tone, but there was this lustful undertone, like the idea brought him entirely too much satisfaction to ignore.

"I was scared you'd say no," I confessed, my body flushing as I laid back on the bed. "I knew if you did, I'd be devastated." It felt vulnerable to be this naked and spread out while confessing my truths like they were sins. A feast for his taking. His laser focus raked over me, scaling over every inch and paying close attention to my pierced cock and nipples. Slowly, he dragged his tongue across his full bottom lip, and it felt like he was praising me without words.

He found me attractive. A throb developed in my groin with that realization. "I haven't had a pet in years," he admitted, giving me his own truth while asking for mine. Our gazes locked together as he kneeled on the bed. There was something so appealing about him being clothed while I was stark naked. His slacks were tight around his thighs, his button-up accentuating every muscle on top of his body.

This dragon had me by the balls and we'd only just met. What would it be like if we met biweekly like he requested?

Would I garner feelings... ones that couldn't exist for a Cupid?

"You're learning quickly," he softly appreciated, his hands drawing up my thighs. The contrast of his blue and my red had a shiver racking my frame.

The bed dipped as his knees boxed me in. It was the closest we'd come to touching, not skin to skin yet somehow just as intimate. "Tell me what you want from this," he rasped, his voice dropping as he eyed me curiously. Again, he asked the hard questions.

He paused, waiting for me. My comfort levels were nonexistent at this point. He unraveled my very armor, expelling all notions of secrecy.

If he knew he did that, he didn't mention it. He gave me moments, expecting an answer, and knowing this was important to him, I relinquished my fear.

"Everything you're willing to give," I brokenly uttered, hating the way my body winced at the confession. My skin prickled with awareness as his wings expanded, widening before my eyes. They were amazing, blue and black, dark in some spots, sharp in others, and so fucking cool.

His eyes didn't leave mine as his left hand gripped my cock. The groan that escaped me was more monster than man.

Twisting at the tip, he shifted his fist, watching me for my reactions. With cockiness in his traitorous eyes, he used his other hand to clasp my balls. "You like this, pet?"

Stars. Fucking stars collected behind my eyes as a grunt escaped from deep within me. It was freeing letting it all flow, not holding back the sounds and reactions. And shit, he ate them up.

He massaged me, pulling and relaxing, all while stroking my tip. I leaked all over his fist while his face filled with satisfaction at every upstroke. "Fuck, you're beautiful," he complimented. The urge to reach him fueled my hands. Lifting one, I nearly caressed his wing—the temptation too urgent to ignore.

He swatted my hand, leaning forward. "Uh-uh," he tutted, his eyes fixated on my mouth. Kissing wasn't off-limits, right? Part of me wanted him to reach forward and lay one on me, the other saner part begged my mind to leave that yearning in the dark recesses of my mind. "Keep your hands to yourself."

The way his words traced my erection as surely as his fist did had me groaning. He had every ounce of my submission. His clothed body stayed above me, demanding my release, and coaxing my full compliance.

"When can I touch you?" I hissed as his thumb pressed into the sensitive underside of me. Our eyes were locked with passion. The urgency in my tone had amusement flitting across his lips.

His hand continued pumping me, my balls screaming to release. I needed it. Between the spankings and the teasing way he tugged on me, everything overwhelmed my senses.

"You can touch me when you're a good little pet and come for me. You'll do that for me, won't you, Valentine?"

I nodded sharply, feeling my pulse race as he leaned forward. His tongue flicked across my nipple, taking it into his mouth as every sensation drove me closer to the edge. He rocked against me, his arousal only further undoing every sense of control I pretended to have. To stop myself from touching him, I gripped the sheets beneath me, needing the leverage.

He didn't stop his movements, if anything, they were more direct, precise, like he wanted me to come at his command, and no sooner.

"Please," I rasped, feeling my chest rise and fall more rapidly as his tongue danced across my chest and tattoos.

"You want to come?" He rose, leaning back onto his heels as he watched me writhe shamelessly. When I didn't offer an answer, he slapped my thigh and I yelped as yearning filled me. My body was overstimulated with every breath that left me, sweat gathering across my back and thighs.

"Yes," I groaned, feeling my heartbeat in my cock and throughout every inch of my body. It rang in my ears, a steady staccato as he observed.

Pyro let go of me, and the type of fussy noise I made resulted in a chuckle from him. His face lowered and before I could ask him why he stopped, wet warmth enveloped my entire length.

"Fuck," I let out, knowing my body couldn't handle much more. "Going to come." He didn't stop as his hand cupped my balls, his tongue stroking each barbell. Pyro sucked as if that were his only mission in life, and he teased as if he'd die without it.

He popped off, leaving the softest kiss on the tip as his eyes roamed over every heated piece of me. "Come for me, pet." He wrapped his fingers around me once more, stroking purposefully, taking my entire length instead of only teasing the tip. The sensation of it all had me shuddering as my orgasm took over. Spurts of my cum released, shooting with my heartbeat across my chest and his hand.

I couldn't even let out a sound as ecstasy overtook every word in my vocabulary, replacing it with grunts and pleas.

"Such a good boy, coming all over my fist." I blinked slowly, Pyro's face coming into clarity as my entire body shook from the aftershocks. He brought his hand to his mouth, his eyes flaming with literal bursts of light as he licked my cum off his palm. "Strawberries, mhmm."

My face flamed. It wasn't news to me that my cum tasted different. Sweet and tangy, and by the expression on Pyro's face, he liked it.

MAEVE BLACK

CHAPTER SIX

PYRO

Valentine - Train

Each time his chest rose and fell, the urge to lick him clean consumed me. Like this, a mess beneath me, heavily breathing, and undone... it was much more than I could've wished for.

"What about you?"

His flushed forehead where curls stuck and sweat trailed downward was by far the best part of this.

"This was about you," I answered honestly, knowing the ache throughout my body would abate as soon as we both calmed. "Remember what I said about after?"

He sighed and nodded. "Tell you what I liked and didn't."

"Precisely," I encouraged, wanting to touch him. Usually, I gave my partners what they needed, but for the first time, coming down from this rush had me wanting skin-to-skin contact, something I didn't offer most unless their aftercare required it. Which my impatient ass forgot to go over his needs. Carelessness was not usual for me, and I'd remedy it.

Out of all the encounters I experienced, only a few ended with me naked and inside them. And never without protection.

Right now, not even a small portion of me wanted to be separated from him, not even by clothing. The high of the scene must've overpowered all sense. Either way, I waited for his response as he controlled his breathing.

"I want to touch you," he began, his eyes flashing with need. "Without your clothes." My cock twitched at his desperation, the way his eyes didn't leave mine, but he continued to keep his hands to himself.

He might struggle with rules and honesty, but he also obeyed so well in all other areas. The way my praise lit him up, unleashing a soft side, intrigued me more than I cared to admit.

"Very well," I rasped, standing up. His gaze tracked my hands, never stopping to look elsewhere. Knowing this tidbit of information, I made a show of undoing every button, slowly. Something about the measured pace had him rising, walking toward me.

"May I?"

With a nod of approval, his fingers slid up my chest. A rumble escaped me, the proprietary part of me enjoying his handling.

Idly, he undid every button, tracing what little skin showed with every release from they eyelets. "This makes me happy, servicing you," he admitted, his tone tender. I gripped his jaw, tilting his face to me.

"I enjoy your honesty."

A small smile curved his lips, making the little metal loops piercing his bottom one move inward. He was stunning. All tattoos and piercings, a fucking sight I could get used to.

After finishing, his hands gripped my shoulders, and the more he touched me, the more intimate this moment felt.

When my shirt slid from my shoulders, he took no time to reach for my pants. His eyes constantly directed back toward me, making sure I didn't want him to stop.

By the time my belt and pants were gone, his face had reddened more, going a deeper color as he appreciated my body.

My cock tented my boxer briefs, and he licked his lips with his wanton perusal. "On the bed," I directed, needing to take the reins back before I lost all sense of control. He retreated, the backs of his knees hitting the mattress. Scooting backward, his spent cock hardened once more.

That's a good pet.

I didn't offer him the praise aloud, but I hoped the way my eyes and nose flared told him so. Because if I spoke right now, I might unravel, and we needed some structure.

Dragging them down my thighs, my length popped free and Valentine's eyes watched every movement. My cock and balls ached, wanting to release, but we both knew it wouldn't be happening quickly.

I kneeled on the bed, coming toward him. The desperate urgency to sink inside him and press into his tightness overwhelmed me, but he stated he'd never been topped before.

Practice and stretching were necessary.

"You didn't tell me what you liked and didn't," I groaned, needing a bit of reprieve and distraction.

He blinked slowly as if he couldn't comprehend why I was speaking and not touching him. With a swallow he closed his eyes. The way his throat tightened brought a little growl out of me.

Opening his eyes immediately, he finally responded, "I didn't like that I couldn't touch you." His words were near a pout and I liked his need for physical contact, it would make the moment we touched that much sweeter.

"And?" I stroked myself lazily, and he couldn't keep his gaze connected to mine.

"I liked that you told me I was doing a good job." He moaned when I circled the head of my cock, licking his lips with desperation.

"How much time do you have, pet?"

His eyes left my cock and met my own. "However long you'd like," he rasped, his teeth digging into the soft flesh of his bottom lip.

"Isn't it Valentine's?" I wondered out loud, noting the day. "Isn't that a big day for Cupid?" An instant eyeroll had me wanting to tease him about misbehaving, but somehow, it charmed me enough to not get me to retaliate.

"Sure, but not for me. I asked for this day off so I could be here and avoid thinking of all that nonsense."

Nonsense?

"What do you mean?" I prodded, needing to know where his mind sat.

"We," he said, gesturing to his chest, "as Cupids create love. We give it to others, and we aren't even allowed to experience it." The absolute bitterness he felt spilled across his expression. "It's not even real." His tone changed, and I immediately knew I was losing him for the moment.

"Guess it's a good thing you're here and can escape." I changed the subject, leaning over him. "Because this is going to take a while, and I need your full attention."

His eyes widened while his face flamed once more, the topic evaded. "Lean back for me," I instructed, watching as he inched backward. His body was unreal, each line and ridge, along with all the art... it appealed to me.

For the first time ever, I wondered what it would be like to switch, to have him inside me rather than taking him. Like him, I'd only ever topped, being taken never appealed to me, but imagining those piercings rubbing across my prostate fascinated me immensely. With a mental shake of my head, I wondered where that line of thinking could go.

"Spread your legs, pet." The instruction came out more of a rasp, a telltale sign my body craved relief. It'd been too long. Since I'd fucked, since I had to restrain myself and contain some sense of control, and this was the first time a partner garnered this type of reaction from me. Not once had my feelings ever become a part of scenes.

Valentine's thighs widened, his feet planted on the bed, his knees spread as well. Beautiful, he was fucking beautiful.

"Can I?" he asked, his hand reaching toward my unclothed chest.

"Yes," I grunted in answer, not knowing how to feel. Usually, I tied up my playmates, even if only their wrists. Keeping them from any form of intimacy. Yet, this creature took every ounce of my idea of platonic and threw it out the fucking window, even if only temporarily.

His fingers dragged down my body, scraping over my nipples and down to the veins leading to my cock.

"You're sexy as fuck," he uttered, licking his lips. "Shit, I just want to lick every inch of you."

I blinked slowly, envisioning him taking my cock down his throat. Not tonight, not while I barely held any control. Slow and torturous, that was the pace we needed.

"And your cock," he said while gulping air. "It's ridged and twisted, like a tree trunk." I chuckled, thinking of how when Arson and I found out our cocks looked like random objects, we joked about it.

I leaned forward, his hands dropping as my mouth hovered his hip. Biting it roughly, I felt my jaw throbbing. Drool pooled, leaking from my lips as it dawned on me... Mating bites were forbidden for Santanas. Until you planned on settling down, they weren't allowed. Even breaking skin at all with teeth could initiate something.

Not once had I ever salivated like this, and I shoved that realization away for later. Instead, I nipped gently at his flesh, watching as he bowed up toward me.

I trailed kisses and swirls of my tongue down until I reached his erection. It was beautiful and tasted like fucking strawberries.

Licking his tip, I slid my tongue along the underside, paying attention to each metallic bar inside him.

He canted upward, his hips flying toward my mouth. I took his entire length, relishing the sweetness of his precum and the remnants from his initial release.

"Pyro," he whimpered, his fingers digging into my slicked hair, messing it up. His hips thrust upward, hitting my throat with every movement. Tracing my fingers up his chest, I pressed my fingers to his lips.

"Suck," I commanded after popping off his erection. He took my fingers into his mouth, sliding his tongue across them, and I noted his tongue rings. Two, parallel to each other. Shit. His mouth would feel phenomenal on my cock.

After dragging my fingers out of his mouth, I pressed one against his hole. He whimpered, and I distracted him with several licks.

Pressing inside him, he moaned and I took his cock in my mouth as his reward. With only one knuckle deep, I pushed upward, wanting to make it good for him.

The way he wiggled and thrust in my mouth guided me to press in more. When he stopped tensing around my finger, I leaned down and drooled onto his hole.

"We'll go slow," I promised. "Then when you're ready, we'll go all the way."

"I want you inside of me," he groaned, demanding, his face glistening with sweat as he clenched down on my finger. "Please."

I pulled out of him and reached for the drawer, knowing they kept lube inside. Grabbing it, I kneeled before him. Pressing his legs upward, I leaned forward and licked a stripe down from his balls to his hole, feathering across with precise movements.

His groan urged me forward, and I continued, laving at him, and making sure to dig my fingertips into his thighs. Knowing that tomorrow, when he was alone, he'd know it was me who marked him. Me who owned him.

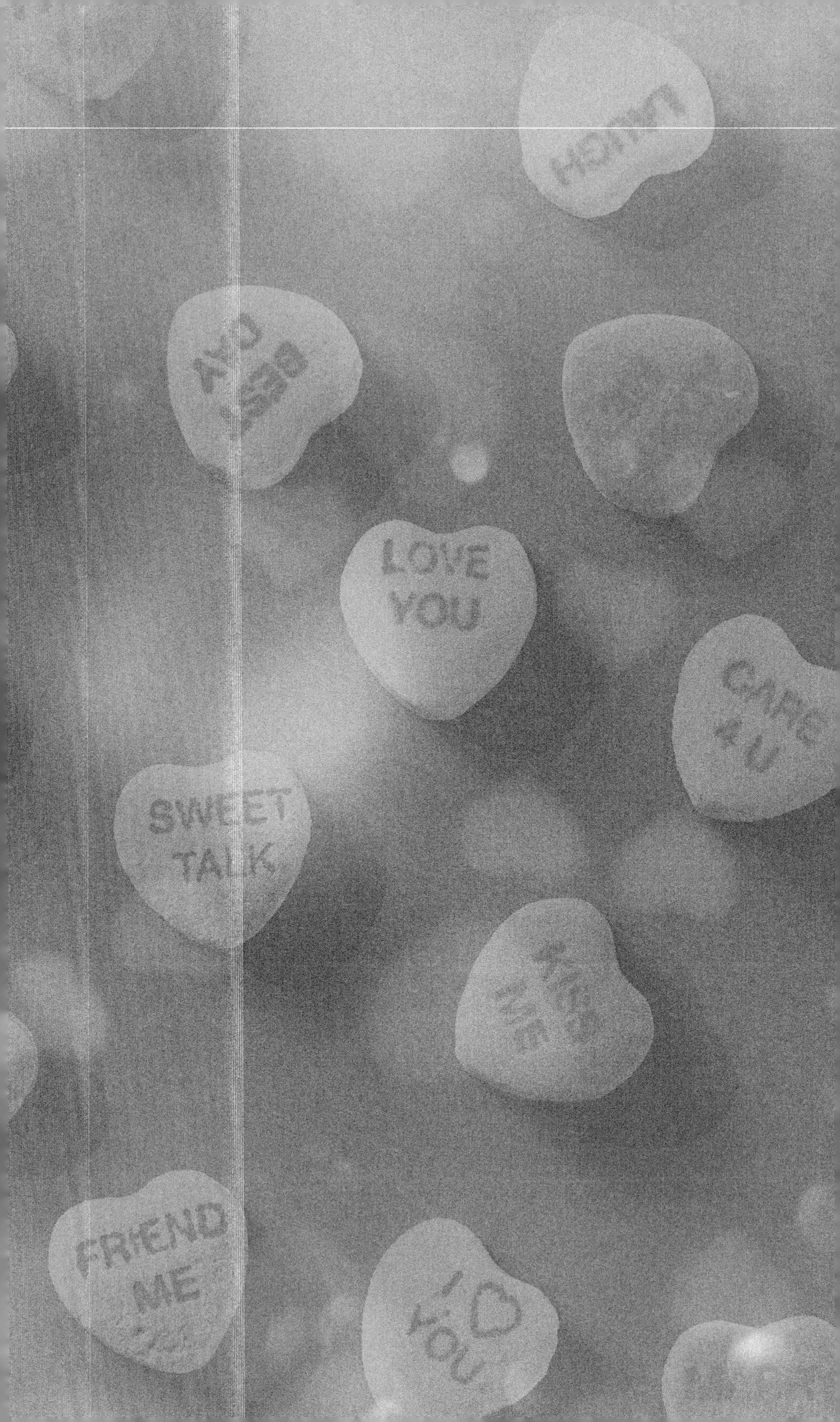
LAUGH
LOVE YOU
CARE 4 U
SWEET TALK
KISS ME
FRIEND ME
I ♥ YOU

CHAPTER SEVEN

VALENTINE

Antologia - Shakira

E very stroke of his tongue eviscerated me. Each swipe winding me up like a little spindle toy, waiting to release and watch me spiral. His finger replaced his tongue, pressing inside me. The pressure built in my balls once more, promising another orgasm, this one would be so much more intense. My dick ached, the kind where numbness overtook and settled deep.

"You take me so well, pet. Do you want another finger?" I nodded enthusiastically, nothing but mumbled whimpers as pleasure sank inside my very marrow.

He scissored his fingers inside me, then leaned forward, sucking me in his mouth. Warm wetness met me and nothing compared to the way he sucked me down, stealing every thought and replacing them with only him.

"I need more." The way my voice dropped to a mere pant had shame tickling my skin. Never had sex felt this way. This intense; this good. Heat swarmed my skin, my stomach, and it even surged across my back.

He released me, his fingers and mouth retreating while he panted. His eyes scanned me, studying my features for any denial. There wouldn't be any. I wanted this, him, and nothing would stop me from feeling it. Logic be damned.

Grabbing the bottle of lube, he stroked his cock, and it was fucking huge. Not only was it daunting to see one so massive near my ass, but knowing he'd be tearing me apart with his words had a new fear lancing through me.

Wetness reached my entrance as he trickled lube over me. "Bear down on me when I start getting in, it'll feel better."

I had no doubt it'd feel amazing just by the way his fingers felt. Ass play scared me for so long, but somehow, I knew Pyro put my pleasure above everything else.

He pressed in with his cock, and the pressure overwhelmed me. Slowly, inch-by-inch, and other than the initial pain, his pausing made it dissipate quickly.

It also helped with his lazy strokes over my erection. I felt so full and he wasn't entirely inside me.

"You're doing so well, taking me. Those little noises you make turn me crazy," he groaned, pressing forward. "You look so fucking good full of me."

My body tensed with pleasure as he held himself inside me. Not moving, just resting. His hands rubbed my thighs, my hips and then my cock once more.

Still, he stayed without moving, and I wanted that more than anything. "Why aren't you moving?" I couldn't help the complaint from leaving my lips.

His smirk told me it was intentional, and then he spread my legs wider. "Warming myself up, pet. Getting all snug."

"Torture," I protested. "I feel so full."

"Begging turns me on, keep going," he rasped, no longer stroking me. I let out a breath, allowing myself to stare at him.

His body couldn't be real, every ridge was defined and blue. He was so fucking blue. His body, unlike mine, was untouched. No piercings, no tattoos, ever the stiff businessman.

"Thirty more seconds, pet, can you handle that?" he asked, breaking me from my appreciative perusal. With a slow nod, I tried to think of anything but the pressure inside me, throbbing against that spot that had me panting.

"I feel like my balls are going to explode." The admission came with a laugh and then he growled.

"Fuck, don't do that," he gritted out, his face one of pain. I squeezed him to get his reaction—and wrong choice.

He slid from me, flipping me over, and before I got the chance to breathe, he slapped my ass twice, then pressed into me.

My body shook as endorphins ran rampant. Sweat clamored across me and his hips hit with every thrust.

"Shit." It came out as a groan while he continued his pace. Pleasure shot from my toes to my balls, and tangled around my abdomen, little tendrils exploding everywhere. "Harder," I begged.

"I think you like punishments," he spoke, the gravelly tone surprising me. "You wanted my cock so buried inside you that you just had to be a brat."

"Yes, yes, yes," I responded, reaching for my dick. It hurt, the ache from the desperation I felt clogging my every thought. Pyro slapped my hand away.

"You come when I say so," he rasped, his pace unrelenting. In retaliation, I squeezed him once more and that's all it took for him to lose control. His body shuddered and he gripped me with ferocious strokes. It took seconds before my orgasm overtook me, making me a shuddering mess as he jolted behind me.

The feel of him releasing surprised me most. The hot heat felt even warmer than expected. It rushed down my thighs as he continued to spill and the scent of cinnamon filled my nose.

His hands gripped my hips as he finished, a few jerky thrusts before collapsing, bringing me with him. Not leaving my skin, he traced patterns on my waist, his nails dragging as he laid kisses across my back.

"You're such a brat," he complained, but he didn't sound angry, if anything it came out as teasing. I nodded, unable to form words. "If I wasn't so spent, I'd punish you."

My body hummed at the concept, knowing I somehow enjoyed it too much. "I can't help myself. It's too good."

"You'll learn, Cupid. Even if I have to paint your ass with bruises."

I liked that idea, a whole fucking lot.

MAEVE BLACK

CHAPTER EIGHT
PYRO

Give Me Love - Ed Sheeran

We up for next week? my text to Valentine read as I sat at my desk.

For the last nearly two weeks, we talked daily. Little things like updates, how each other were doing, and how much we hated slackers in the workplace. It was sweet, a bonding I wasn't expecting.

It didn't occur to me that it became friendlier than that until I thought of not texting him today upset me, so I decided to invite him for our play date and drinks three days earlier than intended. Might not have been my smartest platonic idea, but it definitely made warmth spread across my limbs and lust to seep into my bones.

For once, Arson did as he needed to. Dragging his feet while doing it, but actually following through nonetheless. He shuffled around the shop, praising the workers, their work ethic, and even went and spent time with the drakes, making sure they were appreciated. Unlike us, the drakes couldn't shift between forms. We were their only sense of communication. Being dragons, we could speak their language. We were from Draegyn, a place where dragons originated and existed. Or did, before all the wars and destruction. A vast group of us escaped Darchon during the war of kings.

We took as many drakes as we could save, and now they willingly helped us Santanas, doing whatever we needed.

What do you have in mind? His messaged popped up almost immediately, bringing a smile to my face. Part of me worried I scared him off. While I'd passed out on the bed after we finished, I woke up to him gone.

Nerves ate at me for days, but I told him no attachments, and I couldn't very well act hurt when our agreement was sex based. Not to mention we didn't even follow through with aftercare, and that's a big no-no after any scene. Even if it wasn't super intense the entire time.

You. I sent the text, thinking of the pretty flush that could possibly be covering his face. Valentine turned the best shades of red when embarrassed or shy.

At Vex's?

His question was valid, but something about only going there for our time together every time felt so transactional, so I immediately thought of something else. Something more that I might regret later. It took us from simply sexual to intimate.

No, I think something simpler might be fun. Maybe drinks and see where that leads us?

I wondered if that sounded past platonic, but friends went for drinks, right? Fuck buddies, even. We could keep our agreement and not be confined to only a sex room. Maybe we'd get to know each other more this way.

A weird feeling settled in my abdomen, telling me it wasn't that simple. Nothing was ever black and white, let alone easy.

Oh, I know a place if you don't mind realm traveling.

Realm traveling? He never told me what he did as a Cupid, and there wasn't really a definitive answer unless you were privy. If he was speaking realm travel, he must've had a pretty lucrative career. Hell, he didn't know I was a Santa-to-be. Did he know Santa even existed?

I chuckled to myself, wondering if he ever pieced together my tree-trunk-shaped dick. It wasn't prickly like a tree, but the ridges definitely helped pleasure him. He didn't complain once—other than to tell me to fuck him harder.

You're on.

As soon as I clicked Send, a knock sounded at my door. "Come in!" I hollered, knowing if I didn't they wouldn't be able to hear me over the Christmas music playing in the corridors twenty-four seven.

"Brother," Blaze announced, his deep mustard skin somehow shinier than normal. My brother was the epitome of a playboy. The man could pamper himself with every single thing, yet he couldn't stop himself from dicking anything with legs.

"Blaze," I responded, going over the list of things we needed to do by March. He sauntered toward me, even if I could only see him from over my reading glasses.

"You're always so happy to see me," he sardonically replied, and I set down the list, staring up at him. He wore sunglasses. Sunglasses inside a dimly lit room, for no reason.

"What's with the shades?"

"Oh, these?" he questioned, nervousness leaking through his expression. Much like Arson, Blaze had no sense of time, direction, or even discretion. Like my other two brothers, he was tatted and pierced all over. The only one in this family with decorum for the business was me. He bit his lip and removed them, revealing a black eye.

"Who did you fuck over this time?" I wondered aloud, thinking of all the possible creatures he pissed off in the past, and maybe another to add to the growing list.

"They didn't tell me they had a partner," he mumbled, running a hand through his dark, nearly black hair. "Just grateful the guy didn't rip out my eyebrow piercing with his punch. He hit hard as hell."

"Obviously," I said, pointing to his black eye with disappointment.

He scoffed, coming closer to my desk. "It's not my fault you're a tight ass and want to be the next Santa. I won't be Santa for at least a millennium."

"Knowing you, you'll fuck your way into a marriage before that happens," I rumbled, grabbing the pen and signing off on the new budget for a new table saw, along with many other items we'd need replacing this year.

He let out a hiss and I allotted him my attention. "You're always treating me like a child. You're so uptight," he complained.

"Why are you here?" I deflected, unwilling to feed into his tantrum. Every time I gave in to him, he did something to disappoint me. Was I too harsh on my kid brothers who enjoyed their time while I bitterly couldn't? Sure.

No matter what, if no one gave them tough love, would they ever mature?

"Forget it," he sulked, turning toward the door. Before he left, I let out an elongated sigh.

"I'm sorry," I apologized, feeling that similar rage sinking beneath my skin. "What do you need?"

His face held contempt, the sneer still present on his face. "Dad and Mom haven't been around, and when are they ever..." he muttered the last part under his breath. "I really just need to find Cinder. He's been off-world for so long, I'm getting worried."

My mind traveled to my youngest brother, Cinder. He was a cheeky shit, someone who couldn't avoid being a menace to any society he found himself hanging around. Much like Blaze, he was even further from maturity than him. Their priorities were skewed and that chip on my shoulder reminded me they weren't me and never would be.

Cinder was the baby, our parents gave him all the leeway growing up, and as the most mature brother, it wasn't a shock Blaze came to me.

"I'll phone around," I responded. "Last I spoke to him, he was on *Espegyal.*"

"The monster realm?" he questioned with concern. It wasn't a place us barely-monsters went. We were basically pretty boys to them. That place was filled to the brim with monsters who didn't appear human in any way. The only reasoning for going there was trouble.

I nodded. "He assured me it was a short trip."

"It's been months, Pyro."

He wasn't wrong, but much like Darchon, time didn't work the same there. He could literally have been there for mere hours. Earth worked on a three-sixty-five schedule. One of the only realms that did.

There was *Sin,* the planet where the rotation existed in seventy-two days. That was an entire year there, where life passed quickly. The only reason to go there was to visit the Fates. And going there didn't promise you anything but hopelessness.

"*Espegyal* might have a weird time, it's not Earth."

"He always texts me," he argued, his eyes brimming with unease. Unlike me and Arson, our brother's eyes were brown. Entirely. Like a crocodile's. Right now, they mimicked a depthless hole of despair. He and Cinder were far closer than me and them both. They were like Arson and I, thick as thieves.

"I can force him back," I replied, knowing there was a specific type of magic that pulled him to us immediately, almost like him scraping his hands to stay before the ground cracked beneath and sucked him through. "He won't forgive you, though, especially if he's doing anything special."

Blaze closed his eyes, unleashed fury there. It sucked being helpless, and the magic that forced a Santana here didn't feel good. It knocked you off your ass for days on end, if not weeks. It was the equivalent of putting us in a snow globe and shaking it until we fell from the sky like snow.

"You're right."

"If he's not back and you have any type of gut feeling that something's awry, I'll handle it. I'll even reach out and text you if something changes," I offered, wanting to see him ease back into his careless self.

Seeing Blaze anxious set off alarm bells. First a black eye and then a missing sibling. There was something he wasn't telling me and if he tried with subtle references, I couldn't read his mind.

He needed to be honest.

Which brought me back to Valentine. My family brought out this mistrust. The lies and sabotage each sibling did over the last thousand years tired me out. They lied more than they divulged, constantly living in that forced me to expect honesty in all aspects I could control.

"Try to take care," I attempted one last time when Blaze didn't say a thing. He shook from head to toe as his eyes blazed with smoke. He was seconds from blowing a gasket. Before I could attempt to remedy the situation, his rage overtook him and he flew out of the skylight.

Glass crashed around me, filling me with unease. My brothers would be the end of me.

MAEVE BLACK

LAUGH
BEST DAY
LOVE YOU
CARE 4 U
SWEET TALK
KISS ME
FRIEND ME
I ♥ YOU

CHAPTER NINE

VALENTINE

La Santa - Bad Bunny & Daddy Yankee

"Where are you going with a smile?" Xó teased, her eyes lighting up with hope. She couldn't get it in her head that I could have feelings. So, I erased the look.

"Coffee," I answered, thinking of how much I hated it. The lie was bad, even I knew that. Immediately, her left eyebrow shot up with suspicion and I shrugged it off. "I wanted to try something new."

"You loathe coffee," she muttered, tapping her mug of hot chocolate. My sister lived on sweets. Especially sugary coffee.

I preferred tea, the subtle richness of the flavor consumed in a pleasant way. It didn't overwhelm me with bitterness or the strength of something that didn't appeal to my taste buds.

"Yeah, okay," she muttered with the funniest expression on her face. "When you're ready to divulge your secret, you know where I'll be."

"Yeah, living in your dreams where Christmas is every single day," I groaned, thinking of her obsession with that holiday. Besides the notion that love was more than magic, she believed Christmas to be the best season invented.

She was wrong.

The best holiday is and always will be Halloween.

Anyone who argued could get fucked.

"I've got to head out," I told her, avoiding the fact that being late was a rule Xóchitl would have me break with her questioning.

"Find me if you need anything," she tacked on, a knowing look building behind her pink gaze. We were close, she told me everything and I let her believe I did the same. The difference being, her comfort for confiding in me didn't reflect my own with her. I always felt like the older brother, her protector, and sharing my woes seemed to stress her out and being a burden would never be on my tombstone.

Immortal humor, we don't die.

My mind couldn't focus on that, I was already behind schedule. I couldn't imagine how Pyro would punish me for it, but a thrill shot up my spine at the thought. He wasn't wrong when he mentioned pleasure being a part of pain. When he hurt me, I craved more, and that realization didn't scare me at all, it called to me, giving me hope.

He'd texted me later in the day to meet at Vex's just for a point of contact, and then we'd travel off-world.

This entire concept of meeting outside of the place blurred lines for me. Mentally, I knew it was so he could be my *friend* upon my request, but the other part I didn't give much credit to wanted it to be a desire to be around me.

I held the cuff given to me. Right outside the fuzzy door, Pyro leaned against the brick building, his body calm and ever stoic.

He was beautiful outside of our play time. The way he held himself together, as if it were as simple as breathing, whereas I struggled to keep my emotions in check. There was not a single being who made my knees weak, yet this monster did.

Not being able to express myself usually suffocated me on a daily basis, but seeing his casual demeanor as he waited for my arrival brought me a sense of calm.

"You're late," he chided, checking his watch. Only by seven minutes, I barely got home in time to grab my shit and go.

"My sister—"

He pushed from the wall, tipping my chin. "Uh-uh," he teasingly tutted. "No excuses, pet. Punishments are to keep us both in line."

I shivered at the dark tone of his voice, how it dropped as if he switched into Dom mode. Nodding, my body felt every buzz of our closeness, almost drunken with the feeling. My skin craved his warmth, and the pinching in my chest would be ignored all the same.

"What was your idea?" he changed the subject as I let out a shuddering breath, needing the distance. He overtook every sense when nearby. It felt far more than friendly and less than lovers somehow, but I didn't know how to feel about it in the grand scheme of things.

"There's a place out in Darchon, a place where fae and monsters have a safe spot where wars don't exist, but drinks and dancing are the norm," I explained, thinking of *Vivere*.

His eyes darkened and acknowledgement flickered there too. "*Vivere*," he echoed, his palm sliding down my hip, gripping it. It was almost familiar, like he couldn't help to touch me, but he noticed and dropped it. "I haven't been there in ages."

Did he feel it too—this closeness building far too quickly?

"Darchon isn't exactly a happy place," I quickly noted. Our family only went there when required, avoiding it otherwise.

Something about a club that was for the sole purpose of monsters seemed like a safe bet in comparison to a human one where we'd have to lie about being cosplayers or glimmer our appearance.

Grabbing his hand, I let out a breath, directing a portal with words. Being a Cupid had its perks, our magic wasn't massive, but it allowed realm traveling and things of merriment.

When we shuttered through the veil, we appeared in Darchon, outside of Vivere. Arriving here would make you think we were in a place without technology.

It wasn't incorrect. Most of Darchon lived within the old means, and *Vivere*, along with a few other monster hotspots, didn't. They had technology, things that felt almost science fiction with their grandeur.

We didn't touch as we walked in. We were friends. Friends who fucked, nothing more. I let out a breath, knowing that was for the best. The place was dark, sleek, lit only by dim lights in the sitting area and neon ones in the area where you'd go to dance.

"Val!" Oscar called out, noting me as soon as we reached the main area. His eyes roamed over me, reminding me it had been ages since we'd last seen each other. My spine straightened with curiosity as I peered at Pyro. Disinterest in every definition coated his features. We were friends. Friends didn't get jealous of other friends.

Oscar and I were friends too, except we were friends who *didn't* fuck. That was an important distinction.

"Oscar, this is Pyro. Pyro, this is Oscar."

"A dragon?" Oscar nearly went nuclear with interest. "I thought they were all gone."

"Oh yeah, that's how to introduce yourself," I scoffed, trying to tamper down the jealousy licking my heart with barbed edges. Oscar was a flirt, simply put. Him appreciatively perusing my date—*friend*—irked me to no end. "Let's just talk about the death rate of creatures with subtlety." The mocking and chastising way I said the final words baffled me. It was both with protectiveness and annoyance. And I knew if it were anyone else it wouldn't have mattered. But something about it being Pyro bothered me.

"It's fine," Pyro reasoned, his face filled with amusement. He gripped my arm momentarily, a little squeeze of reassurance. "Yes, I'm from Draegyn."

Even my eyes widened at that tidbit of knowledge. That meant, like me, he was from Darchon. Our gazed connected and something passed between us. Unspoken.

"Drinks?" I evaded, hating the break of connection but needing it all the same.

Pyro silently nodded, and I rushed to sidestep him, needing distance. I thought when inviting him out, we could hang out, and then if it led to more, that would be fine. A schedule. Friends. Possible fucking. *Simple*. Not complicated at all.

My stomach clenched as I realized what outside of fucking did to people. They grew attached, garnered more than simple lust and itches to scratch. The little attention glutton inside me hoped for so much more than little moments and I hate that stupid part of me.

"Valentine, dear!" Cyla hollered over the pounding music. They were a fairy, very goth, and extra humorous. We'd known each other for a long time, and it surprised me that Darchon wasn't much different than my last visit.

"Cyla, how's it going?" Amusement danced across their expression as they dragged a towel over the bartop.

"The same old," they answered. "Your regular?"

"Is it a regular if I haven't been here in five years?"

"Five years?" they mocked with a laugh. "It's been months in immortal time, darling. You forget." I chuckled with a nod.

"You're right, it feels so much longer for me." *In the human realm*, I wanted to say. With Pyro in my head, I decided on something I thought he'd appreciate. "I'll take a glass of meinshine and a tumbler of your best vesper."

Vesper was made from vesperis leaves, something that had both a suppressant and healing affect. When healthy, it made you feel lighter, more at ease. Meinshine was our equivalent to moonshine and wine. Sweet, bitter, but packed a hell of a punch. Maybe it would make me erase the desperation cloying to my heart like a film.

They nodded, grabbing the ingredients, and mixing them. What felt like ten minutes seemed to only be a couple, because Pyro still spoke with Oscar, not acting as if I left at all. I gave Cyla a tip, and waved goodbye, before heading back to my... what was he? A date? Just friends. Yes, just friends.

Nudging his shoulder, I offered the glass, erasing the word date from my mental dictionary. His lips curved at the gesture as he raised his eyebrow. "Only one drink, pet. Can't have you distracted."

Pet. And just like that, my dick strained against my jeans while my heart tried escaping from my chest. I knew the rules at Vex, but I didn't take into account that he'd want them followed outside of there. This was technically our meetup, even if a few days early.

Taking a big gulp, I agreed, ignoring the intrigue from my old friend. His eyes nearly drilled into me with questions but I had no answers.

How did I tell people I met a dragon at a play party and decided to have a meetup agreement without the feelings, where only sex was involved?

It'd be easy to convince my sisters, friends, and even strangers, but myself? I was the hardest one to persuade.

Pyro took a sip and hummed, the sound barely audible as the music surrounded us, but I knew with the expression on his face that he enjoyed the sweet flavor.

Nerves urged me to drink my own, and knowing it was my only one didn't stop me from drinking it too quickly. It calmed me in a way that Pyro couldn't.

Sure, when he controlled our movements in the bedroom, he set me at ease. But out here, I felt out of my element, unsure of our decided labels, and

I hated even needing them. Oscar eyed me suspiciously, and while we hadn't spoken in a long time, he didn't act as such. "Want to dance and tell me how life has been?"

I was about to say yes, needing a breather from the giant dragon next to me, but Pyro shook his head. "He's going to dance with me," he claimed, his voice dark. I didn't know what it meant and didn't understand the way his eyes seemed to be glowing. But fuck, it did something to me, and the more my heart beat in reaction to him terrified me to no end.

With a nod, I handed Oscar my half-gone drink and followed Pyro's moving frame. "What was that?" I asked hurriedly, my skin sweating with unease. We agreed to be friendly, nonchalant, and outside of the bedroom, I *wasn't* his.

He didn't respond but weaved through the bodies. Once he found a little opening, he gripped my hand and pulled me toward him.

His face was mere inches from mine, his one palm on my chin, and the other dangerously close to cupping my ass.

"You can't ignore me forever," I groused, narrowing my eyes. An emotion flickered over his face before he went completely stoic.

"Didn't want to share my time tonight. We agreed it was only you and I while fucking."

The way his mouth traced the word *fucking* had tightness building inside me. He always appeared sure and direct. While I tended to feel on edge with an undercurrent of uncertainty.

"We aren't fucking," I rebutted, earning a little slap on my right ass cheek.

"Not yet," he rasped, his eyes dangerously dark.

"He wasn't—" I argued, but Pyro stopped me by leaning forward and nipping my throat.

"He wanted you, and while it wouldn't bother me if we were only *friends* and not fucking, I won't allow it. Call me irrational, possessive, or even a jealous fuck, but I don't want anyone to touch you, Valentine."

At that, only silence greeted my mind—no music, no noise, just the way his eyes devoured me in a proprietary way, confusing me. *No feelings. No feelings. No feelings.* The chant went on repeat in my brain, wondering why he affected me in this way. We only agreed to this—whatever it is—almost two weeks ago. It shouldn't feel like it meant more to me than any fucking rule I set for my own boundaries.

We swayed to the music, feeling everything and nothing at once. Our bodies moved to the beat but without coordination. We simply existed within the sounds, not thinking too far ahead.

My body felt warm in every sense, and Pyro's always felt like a furnace, heat emanating from him by existing.

Sweat clung to me as we moved in sync, his hands gripping my hips while we rotated. If there was space between us, it wasn't visible.

He danced like he fucked, precise and unswerving, and my body noted the similarities, reacting in the same way.

Pyro's mouth latched onto my throat and I silently groaned. He licked upward, reaching my ear, and when he bit down, I shivered with expectation.

"You're still getting a punishment for being late, pet," he purred in my ear, the vibration nearly causing me to shake. We were charged, energy and fire mixing in a heated battle of control. He turned me, facing away from him, and then he thrust against my ass, and the only thing that appealed to me was feeling him punish me.

When would he realize it did a lot more than correct my behavior? It got me off, it tore me apart and put me together, making me a whimpering mess for him.

"What are you waiting for?" I finally replied, breathing out heavily, wondering how long it'd take before he decided enough was enough.

Gripping my hip, digging his large fingers into my flesh, I groaned at the way I knew it would bruise. He liked to mark me. We might have only had that one night that seemed to go on and on, but he didn't shy away from letting me know that marking me made him happy.

"Wave goodbye, Valentine," he instructed, nodding toward Oscar who stared at us with knowing eyes.

I waved, and within seconds, Pyro guided me outside the club and lifted me. My legs wrapped around his front as he held me. His wings sprang outward, and it took that gesture for me to note he hid them while we were in the club.

We flew above trees and toward an opening. I knew nothing of this part of Darchon, only that darkness met us, and sometimes, that wasn't a good thing.

I didn't push him for answers, something told me he never would purposely put me in harm's way. When we landed, he let me down, and the abrupt loss of his heat was noticed.

He took no time to walk me backward. When my back brushed a tree, he dropped to his knees. That first night he took me, I knew his pleasure never was his goal. He liked watching me fall apart, pulling as many orgasms from me as he could.

Right now, as his eyes watched me heatedly while he hands unbuckled my belt, it told me everything I needed to know.

My pleasure was his pleasure, and he required it.

"Widen your legs," he directed, and I did. My jeans were unbuttoned then, his hands reaching inside roughly, pulling me out. An urgent need to switch our positions nearly had me saying it.

"Punishment?" I reminded him, wondering if he'd fuck my throat for my punishment. The idea of swallowing down his massive cock interested me.

"Your punishment is coming down my throat without being able to touch me," he explained, his burning eyes making me whimper. Pyro knew my need for touch would be an ample punishment.

He stood once more, grabbing my belt and tying my wrists loosely with it. "Be a good boy and keep your arms up. If you reach for me, touch me, or remove your hands, we'll go our separate ways. Understood?"

I nodded, but that wasn't enough for him. He tapped my thigh for my answer. "Yes," I hissed, needing him to touch me if I couldn't touch him.

Lowering to his knees once more, he sucked me down quickly. My arms immediately moved and his incisors clamped down on me in warning. I whimpered as the need to thrust into him grew.

His tongue flicked over his fingers and then he was sliding between my cheeks, thrusting home. I loudly groaned, my entire body shaking as he entered me and sucked in unison. Fisting my own hands, I hoped for some strength. The way my body felt both taut and restless had my legs shaking.

"Please," I whimpered. "Please let me come."

A resounding pop had my gaze flying to him. Even below, all the power rested in those green eyes. The demand for submission, and the offer of pleasure.

"So impatient," he chastised, licking a long streak across the underside of me. "Does my pet want my cock?"

The way my head snapped to nod could be comical if my balls didn't ache with the pent-up need to come. "Yes, I want that."

"Too bad, you're being punished. Giving you my cock would be a reward you have yet to earn." I swallowed the disappointment and acquiesced to his need for this.

"If I'm good..." I started, and paused when his mouth engulfed me. He sought my silence with pleasure. He knew if he got me riled up enough, I wouldn't barter.

It didn't take long for him to swallow me down and when his fingers clamped on my prostate, I felt a pleasure I didn't know existed. He didn't stop as my cum shot down his throat, and if anything, the rumble of him sucking me down told me he quite enjoyed the action.

An emotion tugged at me. Comfort. Something I wasn't allowed to feel. Because it told me I didn't want this to end. Not him topping me and not him being around. That alone scared me. I wanted him. His sighs, his groans, and the contented murmuring into my hair when he thought I was asleep.

We couldn't be more than quick fucks and playmates. Tonight was a mistake and I should've known that based on our daily texts. I grew accustomed to them, needing them to make me smile and get through my workday. This was moving too quickly and breached that friendship we labeled this as. My heart didn't understand what my brain knew to be for the best.

We couldn't extend past every other weekend, no more texts, no more learning what I liked and didn't, and definitely not asking me why I was upset at work and what could he do to help.

Then I thought back to his words of not fucking me, latching onto that as if it were creed. Sure, I knew he wanted inside me, but I also knew I needed to detach immediately. Feelings were something everyone experienced, but feelings where I wanted to meet up with him more than biweekly, that was a problem. I disengaged, even as he fucked into me still.

Worry sliced through me, wondering if he didn't like me like that and whether I was garnering feelings that could never be reciprocated. Cut and run. I needed to fucking run.

"Stop," I rasped, not knowing why I said the words when my body begged otherwise. It needed more. We needed to talk about this, right? About this random fucking shift? It was too quick, too real. His possessiveness along with my comfort. This was fucked up. This couldn't happen.

His mouth released me immediately, his fingers retreating from my body at the same time. "Are you using stop for a safe word or is it a 'stop, it feels too fucking good but continue'? Did I overstep?" His eyes softened, not with anger but pure concern. Something about that look broke a part of me. My mind wandered too quickly. *Fear*. I recognized it immediately. It came and went. The lack of emotional connection with others usually drove it, but when it hit this suddenly, I had to backpedal.

Embarrassment heated my face and I pressed farther against the tree, needing to run.

Run, my mind begged.

My body went into overdrive as I pulled up my jeans and wordlessly rushed away. I didn't know where we were, and Pyro yelling after me didn't stop my legs or stupid heart from beating faster.

Shame as potent as the first time I started to feel things for the random boy I met at the Love Hub coated me, making me nauseous. Feelings weren't real. They were a figment of our imagination. Human in creation. *Not real. Not real. Not real.*

My body shuddered as a drunken stupor clogged every thought. The high of being in the situation with Pyro along with the adrenaline from running in a wooded area that I knew nothing of shook me.

My skin crawled as disgust trampled all my concerns. How could I run like a baby? I knew I always ran. It was my go-to, but not here. Not in a realm my family sought refuge from young, escaping to better my family's life. Not a place that carted more wars and monsters than the monster realm itself.

Pyro's roar in the sky stopped me in my tracks. His voice hollered loudly, impatient, and worried. The flap of his wings echoed in the air like a promise of retribution. Pain rippled through me as I realized how severely I'd just fucked up.

Maybe this agreement between us needed to end. I wasn't cut out for casual scheduled sex. Hookups were more my style. Not knowing their names. Not little tidbits and anecdotes. Just wordless fucks in random places without an exchange of numbers. The power exchange confused my brain too much to be anything more.

This was a sign. It had to be.

With a shuddering breath, I said the words that took me home, knowing leaving him in his current state and me in my own would damage whatever trust we'd gathered.

This was the end of what we'd only started to build.

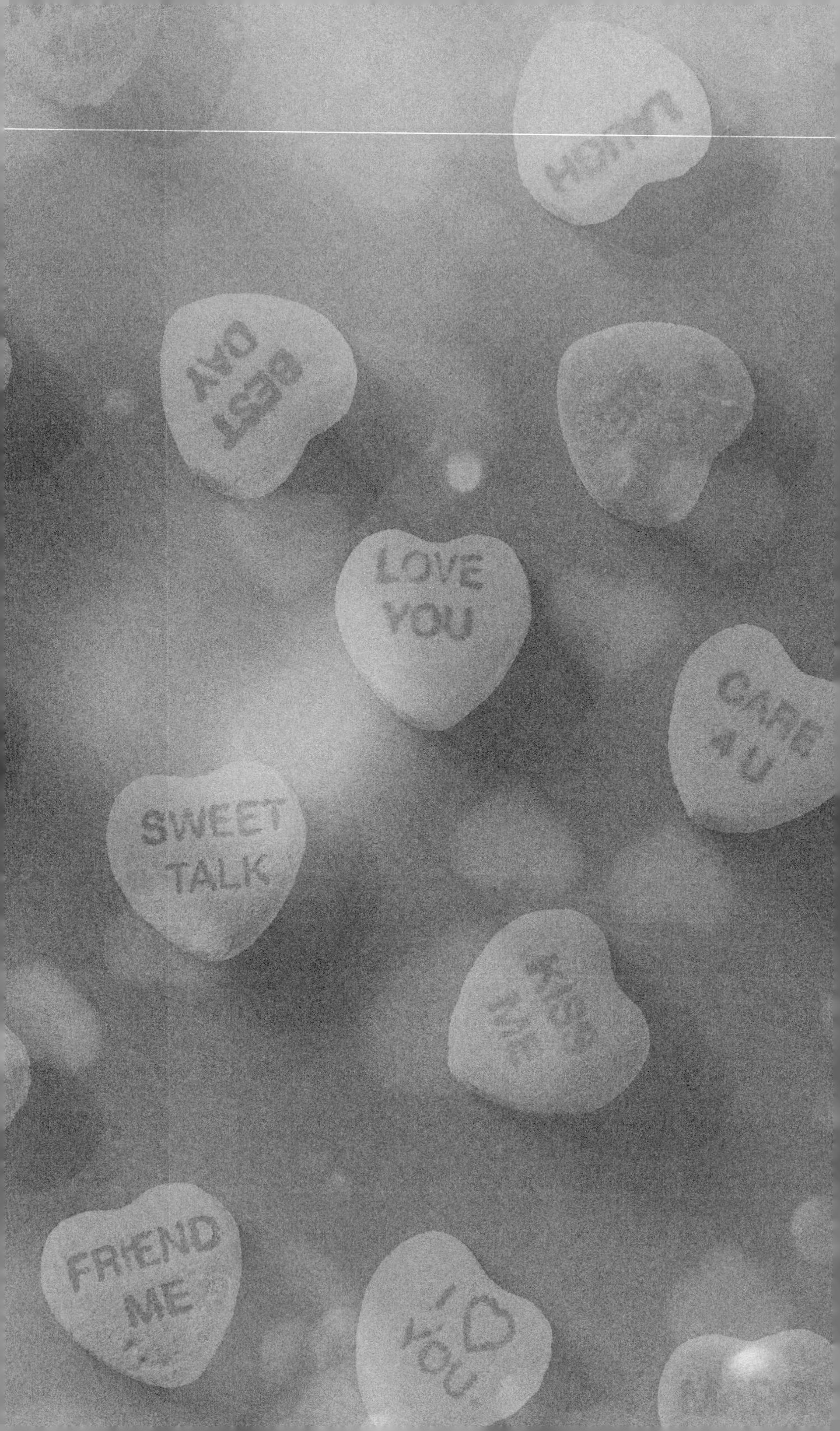
BEST DAY
LOVE YOU
CARE 4 U
SWEET TALK
KISS ME
FRIEND ME

CHAPTER TEN

VALENTINE

The February Following Dear Monster Claus

Déja Vu - Prince Royce & Shakira

I hated weddings.

Not only were they too happy, they didn't make sense in the end. Why spend all this time and money for everyone but yourself?

Bitterness sung inside me, fueling me to paste the scowl on my face. No longer was I softened by naivete. Resentment was my only default now. My Mamá would beat me if she heard me degrading the importance of weddings to our family and our traditions.

"You look beautiful," I admired, ignoring the nagging inside me. My sister was breathtaking. In all her pink glory, she sported a traditional wedding dress, embroidered with bright flowers and patterns that would match Arson's *charro* suit. Mamá insisted we stick to our traditions since Arson did his own privately over New Year's.

Every Cupid had a wedding with *charros* on horseback, leading us down to the event venue. Today, we continued that tradition, even if it went against all rules of Cupids to marry non-Cupid folk. Mamá approved and that was all that mattered.

In her dress, her eyes sad, Xó's stomach was swollen with a child. Cupids didn't give birth—or so they *lied* to us. She was months along and we didn't know when the gestation period for a Cupid-dragon baby started and ended, all we knew was that Valentine's quickly approached and she'd only been pregnant since December.

Yet, she said she felt swollen to the point of pain, and I witnessed humans throughout their pregnancy. She didn't seem like someone who only barely conceived.

"No, I don't," she complained, her eyes shimmering with tears.

"Don't cry, Xóchi, you know I hate when you cry," I gently rumbled, wanting to fix her worry. It bothered me when I couldn't fix those around me with simple words, and most times my pent-up resentment festered too long and anger was my only response. Nothing let me be free like a year ago at this exact time.

"I'm in so much pain and feel overwhelmed and exhausted."

I brushed a loose curl away from her face. She pressed into my palm with a sigh. "I don't feel beautiful, my hair has been falling out for weeks, I can only waddle at this point without pain, and work has been overwhelming with all the new charges. I can't handle this anymore." Her panicked arm movements reminded me of my own mental breakdowns, and I knew if she didn't breathe, she'd fall apart. And while tacos were the best things that fell apart, Xó wouldn't appreciate the sentiment.

"You're stunning, Xóchi. No matter what. Look at your cute belly, you're going to be a mom and everything will be fine?" I posed it as a question, pointing to her, not knowing why it came out that way rather than a statement. "You're basically glowing." Adding that on didn't stop the wobble of her bottom lip or the trailing of tears.

"I feel like a parasite is inside me!" she wallowed, causing me to chuckle, unable to stop it. Everyone experienced pregnancy differently, and the way she didn't seem to be enjoying it made me wonder if our other sisters would be the same when they finally had babies.

If they ever did.

"Joyful," Arson called out, interrupting her angered look leveled at me. His voice deeper than normal, the restraint in his posture reminded me they were soul mates. Made for each other. Apparently, when they bonded, they shared an emotional and physical connection. He experienced everything she did, and he was stressed along with her. Standing there with his traditional *charro* suit, studded, and embroidered to match her dress, he seemed so beat. The strain on his face, even while his eyes were closed, had me respecting him more.

Seeing them didn't change my mind. Love wasn't real for us. These two were just special.

"You're so beautiful, baby," Arson tenderly cajoled, reaching for her.

She whimpered, tears streaming down her face. "How do you know, you can't even see me!" The hysterical way she whined sobered me up. This moment wasn't mine to experience but when I tried to leave Xó, she grabbed my arm. Her eyes glanced at me, stilling me in my spot.

"I don't need to know, my love. You're always beautiful to me. Nothing could change that, and nothing will. But I feel your misery. We can call off the event, we don't have to go out there. Let's get you in a warm bath, where I'll wash your hair and remind you how breathtaking you are."

His eyes still hadn't opened but his eyebrows moved with the emotions scattered on his face. Even I could tell he was weary, living her pain too, he couldn't erase the bags beneath his eyes and the stress lines on his forehead.

"We can't cancel," Xó argued, stomping her foot in a childlike manner. I just wanted to escape this moment and let them decide what to do while I got wasted on tequila.

"Let me help you, baby," he begged, reaching toward her once more. Momentarily, she dropped my arm and let him hold her as she sobbed. "No one matters but you. Whatever you need, let me do it."

She shook her head and then eyed me. "Can you get me Mamá?" The way her face softened as if she needed something only our parents offered. With a nod, I escaped, rushing to find our mom.

Outside the bedroom Xó holed herself up in, Mamá chatted with Dulce and Dion, ease in her shoulders. Mamá was far older than us all, but you couldn't tell by looking at her. Her hair was curly, longer and bouncy, but looser than the rest of ours. Her skin a Haden mango color, with more orange than not, and her eyes were a softer red. She had a beauty mark above her left lip, and unlike me and Dulce, she didn't have piercings. Hell, she didn't approve of ours when we got them. Least of all, my tattoos. A lecture I still got to this day.

She loved us in the way she could, but in moments like these, it was enough. One look in my direction and she excused herself from my sisters.

"Where's *mamita*?" Mamá always babied Xó, she'd always be her little baby, the smallest and sweetest of us all.

"Scared and crying."

She shushed me at the way I didn't inflect as much softness. I did when in the presence of Xó, but didn't show it well otherwise. "Be nice to your sister," she chastised as I led her back to Xó.

As soon as we walked in, Xó whimpered and grabbed her. "Mommy," she sniveled, and I wished I could be more help. Her shoulders shook as Mamá held her, cooing to her reassuringly.

I let out a sigh and pulled Arson with me. "Let's go out there," I directed with a point of my finger. "You've got a crowd to distract."

He grunted, not wanting to leave Xó, but reluctantly followed me.

People waited to walk Arson and Xó. *Charros* on horses, their eyes wandering over to Arson while he put on his dazzling smile.

"It'll be just a moment," he announced, as if he wasn't just falling apart along with her. He was a good man, one who respected my sister and made her happiness his first priority. If only his petulant brother was the same.

I closed my eyes tightly, ignoring the disdain garnered in the last year. It was childish, uncalled for, and all my fault. Yet, I still held Pyro accountable. He could eat glass, for all I cared.

"What was all that about?" Dion snubbed when Arson went to talk to the guests. There were Santanas, Amors, and even some Enamorados too. All the Cupids closest to us and who didn't look down upon their wedding joined.

"She's not feeling well," I offered, not wanting to bring up her hormones. Our sister didn't deserve to be judged by her emotions when they weren't easy to control. She went through a lot in two months. Met the love of her life— which I still thought was somehow a fluke—mated and got pregnant, all while trying to stay a Cupid as the entire Love Hub hassled her for answers.

We had rules.

She broke every one to be with him.

I admired their dedication, and even if their love was a once-in-a-lifetime thing, I didn't fault them for falling.

They matched too well. Her softness and his hardheadedness. They were perfectly imperfect for one another.

"What if her baby is killing her?" she prodded, and I tsked at her.

"Jealousy is unbecoming, Dionysius. Our sister found the love of her life—something unreal and unfounded—and instead of being happy, you're being snide as fuck."

She blinked slowly, her eyebrows near touching her hairline. "Excuse the fuck out of me," she hissed, turning with anger.

Our sisters were the best and worst. When they rose above, their moods reflected that. Sure, they were borderline bullies to most creatures, but they were soft where it counted. Sometimes, that left when their greed overwhelmed them.

Like now.

Dulce was the peace to Dion's chaos. The twins were the opposite of each other and volatile together. Part of me wished love was real just so they could be chill for once in their lives.

Dion stomped away and went directly to Dulce, grumbling in her ear. Dulce turned to me with a disappointed shake of her head and I audibly groaned.

There was no winning with these two.

MAEVE BLACK

CHAPTER ELEVEN
PYRO

Qué Bonito Amor - Vicente Fernandez

My blood froze when he walked outside. Avoiding all unnecessary contact, I hid from Arson, evading this exact moment. As an alternative, I waited with the horsemen and the houseguests waiting to escort Arson and Xó down to the reception.

Blaze and Cinder were even here, even if I had no fucking clue where Cinder had been for the months he disappeared. He rocked an intense scar from the right side of his forehead all the way to the left side of his jaw. I'd ask him about it soon. When my mind could focus on more than the man who stole my soul straight from my body.

Mom and Dad chilled with drinks in their hands, like nothing in the world mattered since they retired. They nodded at me when they caught me staring. I shook inside, wondering why the burdens of this family always came down to what I offered everyone.

Val distracted my thought process, looking so fucking good, his hair curlier than normal, product moisturizing it to make his locks appear more defined, even if a hat covered half his head. He wore jeans with an embroidered button-up tucked in the waist, looking so different. He was a certified bad boy, piercings, tattoos, and an angry frown. Right now, I'd say he looked ever the rugged horseman.

I'd say I've never seen Valentine look this good, but it would be a lie. When he was beneath or above me without clothing came to mind, taking my breath away.

He grabbed something from his pocket, lighting it up with a Zippo a moment after. With his first whiff, his shoulders settled.

I wanted to pull it from his lips and demand answers. Take it and make him promise me not to hurt himself with sticks of whatever kind of chemicals he decided to take. Force him to choke on my cock after apologizing with his tears. Anything to steal back the eleven months I endured without him. But no, what I craved most was to tie him to my bed and mark him, redden his ass, and unleash a near year of unspent anger.

He left me.

Not only in another realm, but at night, where he could've died. We weren't exactly in the safest domain, and he just fucking booked it. The part of me more primitive than logical roared as if someone took what mattered most from me. Not once in my life had I ever felt as helpless as when he rushed away.

At that point, I hadn't understand what it meant.

I did now.

Nothing in the span of that night should've led him to running from me and blocking me from contact. Not knowing where the misstep was ate at me since.

He didn't explain, he didn't give me anything. He tucked, ran, and then never contacted me again. Not even when I saw him at Christmas did any of it make sense. He acted angry *with me*. Like I pushed him away and betrayed him.

Seeing him again unraveled me. If we were alone, I'd have rushed him then. Maybe I would today. Wait until no one hovered, and then pounce.

My body burned as he threw his head back, enjoying whatever he inhaled. His peace was mine. To gather, create, and steal if need be. *No. That left the day he did.*

Right now, he sought refuge in whatever substance took him from his current predicament. I hated that stick he huffed, and it bothered me that he could be so at peace when I'd been a mess since he left.

I always considered myself a controlled monster. Not a man but a heathen wanting to implode, but saving the intensity for my playmates. They helped me as much as I helped them, and since Val, I haven't looked at another being. Not man nor monster.

The unstable way my day-to-day became unraveled me. Since that night, unable to give him aftercare or soothe his worry, whatever caused it. We were doing so good. Our night seemed perfect, and then it changed.

What did I do?

Before I could decide whether to approach him or not, Arson sidled up to me. "Xó's freaking the fuck out," he confessed, his body stiff, finally leaking the anxiety he masked so well.

"She'll be okay," I reassured. She experienced a lot and emotions were haywire when you involved the stress of pregnancy and an entire wedding.

As if he didn't believe me, he rubbed the heels of him palms into his eyes, sighing heavily. With everything in my life, my obligation to fix this settled over me. Since meeting Xó, my brother grew. There was the moment near Christmas where he rushed out, and like Val, he couldn't communicate his wants, but he fixed it. He hadn't left her side since.

They were expecting a baby.

Another possible Santa.

Unease coated my tongue as it swelled with a new wave of acrimony. The hatred and unfairness of my life were married in my mind. In secret, they danced, rejoicing in my downfall. Without my future, what was I?

Nothing.

I was fucking nothing.

Now, Arson decided to stick to being Santa. No Santana had ever mated and continued the tradition of being the man in red. If so, there would never be a new one. No one would ever phase out of the role.

There was no future for me where he broke the one covenant we all agreed to as children. Once we matured, married, and settled down, we created the next lineage of Santana men. The deciding factor was up to each one. Unless you were the firstborn. Like Arson. He was the only one who didn't get a choice, and if he had a son—he wouldn't have a choice either. Would he repeat the mistakes of our parents... force the role upon those who had no desire to continue the family tradition?

He broke all the rules settling down yet staying Santa, taking all my choices away. Without any promise of a future, my life felt directionless, swimming in the middle of the sea without a single ounce of hope for finding land.

With Blaze and Cinder, it was easy. They didn't want the job. But me? I lived my entire life in restraints, holding back living, to become the one thing I always wanted.

Now, that dream ended and I waded into the depths of that blue water, searching for a new thing to latch onto.

I shook my head, wondering where those thoughts came from. *This isn't me.* Sadness wasn't my thing.

"Are you even listening?" Arson griped, pulling my attention from my inner prison. I ran a wary hand through my hair, messing my perfectly gelled locks.

"Sorry, a lot on my mind."

It wasn't untrue. Since Arson came back to work, doing everything he was supposed to... it hurt me. Schedules and itineraries kept me in routine. Without them, I spiraled.

"Yeah, I guess so."

Sparing him a glance, he stared at Val, turning in his direction. He knew something was up with us but instead of poking at it, he silently accepted whatever it was. I'd tell him when and if I ever felt ready.

"You could always tell me as a distraction?" I shook my head.

"Nothing to say. It was a dalliance."

"A dalliance?" he scoffed, rolling his eyes. "You don't look at *dalliances* like you're ready to pin them down."

My mood worsened when Val didn't even look my way. He ground his smoke into the dirt and left, much calmer than the last time he disappeared on me, yet it still stabbed at me.

"I can't tell you what happened between us," I finally admitted, turning to look at my brother. His anxiety lessened, my own issues a salve for his current situation.

"Well, you start with words, they form sentences, and then—"

"You're a pain in the ass," I grumbled, thinking to all the times I offered him the same type of response. "I can't tell you because it doesn't fucking make sense." We were very similar, even through our differences. Arson was me if I ever gave in to my desires, letting caution fuck off.

He was who I'd be if I didn't take Val's running for a safe word.

He was who I'd be if I ran headfirst into the coral devil that shot his fucking arrow through my heart.

But he wasn't me. I wasn't him. And Valentine might have shot me, but like the heartsick monster I was, the festering and unhealed wound existed from my own choices to not move on.

Whatever happened next was on my shoulders.

MAEVE BLACK

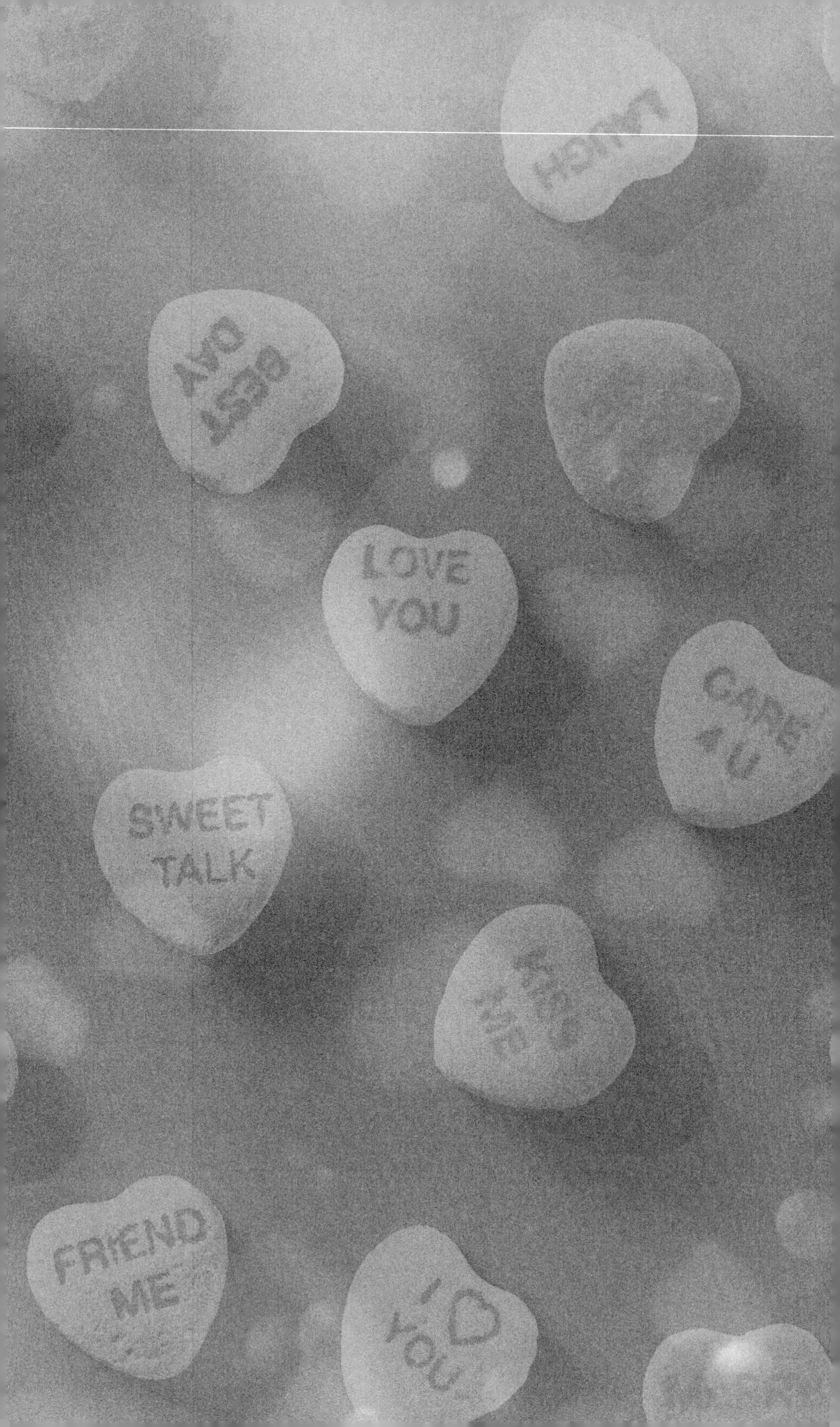
BEST DAY
LOVE YOU
CARE 4 U
SWEET TALK
FRIEND ME

CHAPTER TWELVE

VALENTINE

Donde Esta El Amor - Pablo Alboran ft. Jesse & Joy

My sister finally came out of the bedroom, her tears gone and a newfound piece of hope in her eyes. She married the love of her life with all of us surrounding her. Afterwards, the *charros* lined up, and we all walked toward the after party venue.

We decided to hold this in our hometown. The one in Darchon—the long-hidden city of *Amantes*. Like the shades of conversation hearts, our city was filled with colors. The flowers, our trees, and all the nature felt like an entire village of love.

Pinks, purples, blues, reds, and even greens, all pastel shades surrounded us as we walked. Cupids, outside of our close relatives, threw petals, their love magic dusting the air as they cheered. No one could truly erase culture when you continued it on.

They joined us as we trailed to the barn, the stunning mariachis walking alongside the *charros* as they played, sang, and celebrated.

My sister cried once more, but this time her face didn't appear saddened or stressed. Pain didn't reside in her flushed, wet cheeks, but *love* did.

That four-letter word that still made zero sense to me, I couldn't grasp it, but I knew—I witnessed it with both of my eyes reflected in her own.

She watched everything around her, the turn of her head swiveling to each side of the street as people sent well wishes and cheered for their union.

Nothing mattered when happiness was as ripe as the fruits here. Arson even seemed enamored with the feel of it all. He took it all with ease, knowing our traditions differed from his, but he absorbed them, living them along with us, and making sure Xó experienced it all alongside him. I'd never forget the way he carried her, twirling, and peering in her eyes with an endless type of devotion.

Once the line of people became a massive parade of Cupids, we made it to the venue, decorated in soft pinks and bright reds.

If not for my distaste of Valentine's, I'd find it charming and very fitting to the theme. There were tables all around, leaving the entire center for dancing and mingling. They decorated everything with tulle, glitter, and ribbons. Near the back there was an entire bar with beers, several different tequilas, and even margaritas. Everyone knew shots were a must, a staple even.

Everyone watched as Xó made her way to the front, side by side with Arson. They would be doing *la víbora de la mar*, and when the chairs were brought over by what I guessed were Arson's other brothers, they stood on them.

Knowing my sister would be unstable, I rushed to her, anchoring her legs. Staring down at me, she gave me an appreciative glance. She and Arson held hands, creating a snake-shaped arch. Across from me, near the growing line of people, Pyro stood.

All the air in my lungs left as he sauntered over to his brother, grasping his legs like I did for my sister.

We were anchors, floating in the sea of denial. Held down by hopes, and tugged on by reality. His eyes didn't leave mine as people passed through the arch.

Everyone danced with smiles on their faces, giggling with happiness. Dulce and Dion held hands, gliding beneath the arch with knowing expressions. Dulce eyed me and then Pyro, a smirk tilting at her lips.

Fuck off, I mouthed. A snicker escaped her and she passed through with Dion. My attention redirected at Pyro, and my blood iced over with the promise in his gaze.

People would say he had no expression, reaction, or form. But I knew. In the way his eyes burned for me—*at me*—or whatever the fuck one would call it.

Mamá and Papá came through next. Papá rocked a *charro* suit as well, a deeper purple, similar to his skin tone. My parents made zero sense to me. Sure, Mamá offered us what she could, and Papá never guided us wrong, but in their eyes was a vacancy Xó and Arson didn't reflect, and since their union, I've based all knowledge of love on them.

My parents didn't spent time together outside of appearances. They weren't caught up in each other, smitten, they almost appeared shackled to their fates. Smiles were offered to us kids, big ones, where it reached their eyes, but in their expressions when they twirled together, there was nothing. All a façade.

My eyes drifted back to Pyro who still scanned me, and this time, anger existed there. It was tangible, a rubber band stretched past its threshold, and I was worried for the inevitable snap.

Punishment, his eyes promised.

I closed my eyes, blinking away any residual effects of his

expression, and peered at my sister. The line was nearing its end of dancers, and fatigue set into her features. Glancing at Arson, I could see the same expression, but his had a big wave of concern.

My hand rubbed soft circles over my sister's back, soothing her in whatever way I could as the final dancers went through. Before I could help her down, Arson hopped off his chair, grabbing her bridal style.

Their gazes locked, the type of passion flickering there had envy gnawing deep within me, a cavernous mouth of endless hunger.

"I'll take it from here," Arson uttered, leaning toward me and Pyro. We both grabbed the chairs and the songs ensued. Arson didn't let Xóchi down, he carried her while they did their dance. A non-traditional one where she didn't have to do anything but peer into his eyes.

As soon as I made it to the farthest table near the exit, I set the chair down. Before I could even grasp what my role was in this event, my shirt was gripped and I was dragged soundlessly away out the back door to the barn.

Gathering my wits, I struggled in the arms encasing me. When he let me go, our glares mirrored one another's.

"We had a deal," Pyro bitterly snapped, his angry orbs of heat blazing with disappointment. I didn't think he'd ever call me out on it, but he'd never been the meek type.

"Yeah, and?"

Wrong answer. Definitely the wrong fucking choice of words.

His eyes somehow darkened further, his lips twitching with a sneer his only response. He was pissed, and again, I was the object of all that ire.

He pressed me against the wall outside. The two suns had crested over the valley, growing darker with each passing second. Pyro smelled so smoky, a cinnamon type of spice that settled in my groin far too fucking fast.

"I had three rules." His darkening gaze stripped me bare, digging where it hurt. He saw me. Not the me that felt fine in the presence of others, but the other side that needed his type of dominance. Needed to be called out on my shit and handled without care.

"Three too many," I argued, pushing at his chest. He didn't budge, not even a little. He boxed me in against the slatted wood like a caged animal.

"Valentine," he growled, his control teetering on the edge. But fuck, I couldn't think of anything when he smelled so good.

"What do you want, asshole?" The insult felt bitter leaving my tongue, but he was. He pushed my boundaries and tore apart my composure.

He chuckled, fully, his head thrown back as if it was the funniest thing he ever uttered. When he glanced back at me, only heat reflected there.

"I forgot how big of a fucking brat you are." His words enunciated with our lack of space, the way his chest pressed against mine and left me no room to run. I opened my mouth to respond and felt the retort too easy, not enough snark. "Cat got your tongue, pet?"

Pet.

Fuck me.

I blinked as if he hit me in the face, shock my only response. "Don't call me that," I rushed out, wanting to hide. It was like no time passed, but it had, and I ran.

He pressed into me, his erection matching my own. The thought that he and I both got off on the rush of us only further angered me.

"Why, does it make you hard?" he gravelly asked, his tone too deep. Too fucking sexy. The way he spoke to me in a domineering way that made me a puddle. His hand flattened near my face more, barely distracting me. Anyone could come back here and see us, but I didn't care.

"Fuck you," I hissed, needing space. Between the air filled to the brim with his spicy cinnamon and the heat he emanated by existing, it overpowered everything.

Why did I run?

Why didn't I just give in?

My chest hammered, my palms clamming up as they did every time he invaded my space.

"I bet if I dragged you to those bushes out back and fucked you raw, you'd like that." My dick throbbed with his words, yet anger drove me to turn my face. He gripped my jaw, forcing our attention to each other. "I bet your cock is even leaking for me, pet. I bet for the last eleven months, you fucked your fist thinking of how I made you come harder than you ever have before."

"I hate you." I grimaced at the lie, my body pulsing with need.

"You don't," he taunted, trailing his nose up the side of my face. It was feral, all raw like an animal marking its territory. "You can lie to yourself, to your friends, and even to your family. But don't fucking start lying to me now."

My chest ached, he hit the nail on the fucking head every time. I didn't hate him, I couldn't. He unraveled me.

I pushed him again, needing the distance. This time he let me, but not before leaning into my ear. "You're mine, Cupid. Today, tomorrow, and every day after that. You will kneel for me again, and I'll prove to you that running is fruitless."

With a gulp, I pushed past him, escaping him as far as my legs would take me. This wasn't supposed to happen. The fact that our paths are forever crossing scared me.

I couldn't do this, let alone fight it.

MAEVE BLACK

CHAPTER THIRTEEN

PYRO

Solo de Mi - Bad Bunny

I lost it.

That string that kept me tethered to sanity, it frayed, leaving only anger and desperation in its wake. We had a deal, and he fucking reneged on it.

I adjusted myself and headed back inside to let Arson know I'd be leaving. Between him taking my Santa spot and losing all sense of life, I needed to breathe.

Valentine wound me up, not even purposefully. His very existence promised me pain and disappointment, yet for eleven months all I thought about was saving him. I couldn't escape this weird concept of holding him, forcing him to see his accomplishments, and praising him every step of the way.

Who'd have thought that nearly a year ago, taking him on two little sexual excursions would lead us to this anger and doubt.

In those eleven months, doubt didn't exist or linger, and I mentally plotted how I'd find him once more. Fate was funny in that sense, leading us together by marrying our siblings.

There was a part of me that felt snubbed, but that didn't drive me to pinning him on the barn's wall, no, it was the festering ache he created when he opened up to me.

Instead of running into Arson, I bumped into his wife.

"Pyro, hi!" she said on an anxious laugh. Pain etched wrinkles on her forehead, a telltale sign she needed to sit down.

"Let's sit," I offered, and appreciation lit up her expression. We sat while Arson still took dances from everyone. Instead of pinning money, they pinned words of affirmation, things that would be helpful in their marriage. Little tidbits, jokes, and even some family recipes.

Xóchitl let out a heady breath, her smile a little forced. "I was meaning to speak with you all night, but I've been a little emotional."

"Don't even stress," I reassured her, remembering how Arson was earlier. "What's up?"

She frowned a little and then grabbed my hand. Hers seemed cold, clammy, almost worrisome.

"I'm really struggling with my charges," she said, her eyes brimming with tears. "Like to the point that I'm in constant pain and am upsetting the other Cupids. People are missing their fated dates, and it's starting to wear Val out."

I wanted to tell her it was okay, that she was pregnant and stressed, that nothing could be controlled like that and Valentine could handle his own, but she hurried to continue.

"I know you haven't told Arson, and won't, but it's plainly obvious to me."

"What do you mean?" I offered the only ounce of nonchalance

I could. Whether she somehow knew how deep these feelings for her brother went or the fact that I was lost, she didn't say. She simply offered me a small, knowing smile and patted my hand reassuringly.

"Arson told me you convinced him to read my letters, that you always were the person who handled everything. He explained that you carried the entire world on your shoulders, and he never knew how to thank you."

Emotion clogged my throat at her words, making it nearly impossible to breathe. All the anger festering from my encounter with Val dissipated simply from knowing my brother saw me in some way. He acknowledged what I did for him, even if he only told her and not me.

"I know it's not easy seeing him take the role as Santa, even now."

Our gazes connected and I knew I'd given my entire life away with whatever my expression showed because she nodded as if she was right, yet I hadn't said a single word.

"Until you find your footing again, I need you to help me with something." Purpose became apparent in her words. Since leaving the North Pole on Christmas, I hadn't done anything but stew. Dwell on Val and drown in the realization that I wasn't needed anymore.

Xóchitl gave Arson the hope and spirit he missed, and he didn't even need my push to get things done.

"Anything," I finally offered, noting her waiting expression, allowing me to take in her words.

"Be Cupid for me. For a little while, at least. My numbers are low and while the Love Hub hasn't shunned me entirely, they don't offer me help or lessen my load. When there's an imbalance with love and hate, the world grows darker. It might sound silly, but the more hatred that overpowers love, it makes us all suffer."

It didn't make sense, not really, but I nodded.

"I need you to do what I do. I'm not sure how to imbue you with my magic, 'the love touch.'" She put quotations over the words. "But I know the old-fashioned way before magic happened works too."

"That sounds horrific," I muttered quietly, thinking of not having a charmed buffer for these things.

Her light laughter filled my ears and she shook her head. "It's not terribly hard, but I'll see about the magic. I've heard of Cupids being born without it and receiving it later in life… maybe whatever that is will help you."

"I don't think—"

"Shh," she silenced me with a shake of her head. "You *can* do this. It'll help me, and give you a distraction." She stood, her eyes glimmering with something akin to hope. "Valentine needs some competition. It's two weeks before Valentine's Day. He wins the rush every single time. Maybe you can knock him off his pedestal."

Challenge accepted.

My eyebrows rose of their own accord, and the grin that escaped me couldn't be hidden either. "Now, you've definitely convinced me."

"I knew it," she whispered conspiratorially. I eyed her.

"Knew what?"

"Nothing," she returned with a smirk, the pain from earlier seemingly passed. "I'll have Arson send you the coordinates for the Love Hub."

With a nod of affirmation, she waddled off toward her husband. But across the venue, where tequila was being taken in rounds of shots, stood

Valentine. His eyes narrowed at me and I knew he wanted to punch me.

Outside only proved to me that he wanted me badly, and if I had to convince him of what we could have, I would.

After all, I had nothing to lose anymore.

Dating, love, and fucking? On the table—and no more platonic bullshit. I'd make him mine, even if he fought me every step of the way.

LAUGH
BEST DAY
LOVE YOU
CARE 4 U
SWEET TALK
KISS ME
FRIEND ME
I ♥ YOU

CHAPTER FOURTEEN

VALENTINE

Work Song - Hozier

"Love is in the air..." Paloma announced, waving around a stack of everyone's next charges.

"Don't get that shit on me," I grumbled, violently waving my hands in front of me.

"Funny, Val. Absolutely hilarious," she mocked, tapping her red nail on the stack she gave me. She divided them, adding extra to my pile, knowing I'd get through mine far faster than anyone else.

Everyone stayed with their jobs, making sure it all panned out. I did not. There wasn't an ounce of me that craved watching them fall from a magical touch.

Not once had one of my jobs failed, they never divorced, and they stayed together forever. Which to me, meant everyone wasted precious time on being sappy lovesick fools.

Everyone's chairs swiveled somewhere behind me. "And for you, Mr. Santana," she flirted, more than likely handing him papers. Turning in my seat, my stomach dropped. Her infatuated look was aimed at the man who haunted my nightmares.

Fuck right off.

"Thank you," he paused, not knowing her name, but being charming all the same.

"Paloma," she answered.

"Paloma," he purred, giving her a wink. He did it to piss me off, because he didn't even look at her when he took the papers from her hand. If anything, he avoided touching her fingers and made sure I knew it was *me* he sought a reaction from.

Well played, asshole.

I glowered and turned away from him, immediately shuffling my own stack like tarot cards, allowing the Fates to decide who I dedicated my time to first.

"Val," Paloma singsonged, interrupting my peace. I let out a little huff, more than annoyed that she flirted with the man I wanted nothing to do with.

"Yes, Omi?" I sarcastically responded.

When she didn't immediately go into a spiel about being kind to coworkers and teamwork makes the dream work, I rotated. Standing next to her was the bane of my existence. *Pyro fucking Santana.*

"Your sister asked Pyro here to take over her workload until after the baby arrives," she explained, motioning at him like he was a piece of art. He was, but she didn't have to remind me. "Since you are our best Cupid, he's going to shadow you."

"The fuck he is," I growled. Her eyes widened, not usually hearing that type of disdain from me. The fucker's lips twitched with amusement as Omi's mouth stayed open.

"Don't make me go to HR, Val. Your mom would smack you."

Thinking of my mamá and her pension for *chancla* throwing had a shudder running through me. "You're right, my apologies. My comment still stands, though."

She rolled her eyes, touching Pyro's shoulder to direct him closer. But fuck, I couldn't see past the fact that her hand touched him or understand why I gave a single fuck.

She smacked me with a stack of paper. "What. Is. Wrong. With. You?" She enunciated each word with a swish of the paper to my head.

Chuckling, I imagined this was much nicer than what my mamá would have done as a result of my insolence. "Okay, okay."

"That's right," she tutted confidently, walking away with a straight spine. "Get to work!" She made sure to holler loud enough to make me flinch before she disappeared out of sight.

Turning toward Pyro, humor lined his smile. Well, fuck him, and fuck his perfect smile. "I hate you."

"Keep telling yourself that, pet. Maybe it'll make fucking you that much hotter."

I groaned audibly, standing with my first assignment. "We're going to the human realm, try not to hover too much." With an aggravating smile, Pyro followed after me, his body close behind as I breathed in his spice. If I could absorb how he smelled and put it into a tea, I would. He'd be the most fantastic flavor.

We appeared in a place I hadn't yet been. Somewhere warm with a desert-like climate. In front of us, a lone store existed, and I already knew being in a fairly uninhabited place for the next couple days with Pyro would grate on my nerves.

It took at least three days to find who the second person was. Unfortunately, we were only given one of the names in most cases, where they worked, and why they were fated.

Pyro trailed behind me as I made my way to the store. It was bigger than a convenience store but smaller than a supermarket. It looked like it could use some TLC for sure.

"How are we supposed to look?" Pyro whispered in my ear, far too close for comfort. I flinched, nearly jumping from the heat.

"A glamour," I answered, then recalled he wasn't a Cupid. Letting out a sigh, I gripped his hand. But I didn't intertwine our fingers. This was necessary, not intimacy.

He lifted both of our hands, studying the awkward way I grasped him. "I always knew you were the handholding type," he teased. I let out a snort, not because he was funny, but as a result of him saying the words without a single expression on his face.

How did one tease with an indifferent expression?

"Can't have you visible to humans," I retorted, wanting to keep my distance. He made me feel things, and no one wanted to feel less than me.

The door automatically opened for someone and we rushed through behind them, making sure we didn't get hit. Sensors couldn't always detect us when we were glamoured, which helped when sneaking into forbidden areas, and sucked when sliding doors randomly hit you.

Inside there was one cashier, a bag person assisting, and a few people milling around the aisles. I scanned for the woman on my sheet. Her description listed her hair as black, long, slick-straight, and that she wore glasses that didn't quite fit her face. She was adorable in a quirky kind of way.

How Pyro stood by my side should have bothered me, his proximity almost more than friendly, but with his hand in mine, I couldn't think straight.

It confused me. Letting that thought trail off, I finally found her name, distracted by the silent dragon looming next to me.

"Her name is Ruby, she works on the store's inventory team, and hardly leaves her house for more than the mundane nine-to-five," I described, reading over her file to Pyro. I wish people could see how they wasted away when they didn't allow themselves to experience things, but like the others, she lived a pattern of bland sadness I knew all too well.

"She seems so lonely," I tacked on, not realizing my thoughts were vocal. A tender squeeze to my palm stopped me in my tracks.

"You may have everyone else fooled about how you feel when doing this," Pyro acknowledged, gesturing to the paper. "But I can tell you care." He tapped my chest, right above my frantic heartbeat as we rounded the aisle she currently worked on.

His eyes narrowed at me before widening with suspicion, but I couldn't stop thinking about how he acted when I had a job to do. He could pretend to know me all he wanted, but the truth was that I didn't even know myself. So, I avoided anything remotely similar to acting the right way just to be who I believed the Cupids wanted.

"No more talking," I scolded, wanting nothing more than to escape the way he dissected me as if I were under the knife, and he tried to find the diseased parts of me to remove and clean.

"If I stop talking, will you admit you're scared?"

"I'm not scared," I admonished, shaking my head. Where did he get off?

He stopped me, gripping my hand tighter than before, twining our fingers together this time. The people didn't notice us as he dragged me toward the back of the store—thankfully glamours worked with both noise and visuals. He pushed the door open with a kick of his foot, not waiting for my acceptance. Heat boiled my blood, not with anger but desperation. We avoided this exact conversation for nearly a year, and now we were here. A place I couldn't exactly escape from.

As if to distract me, his fingers traced my rings, a calming gesture he might not even realize he offered. He didn't stop even as he directed me away from prying eyes. Not that anyone could see us, but the sentiment was still there.

I knew I should stop him, but this couldn't go anywhere. I wanted it to, and I still followed in hopes he'd fix the broken parts of me.

Pyro's anger tickled my senses as he pressed me against the wall. I found myself amused with how we always found ourselves in this position. He demanded my truths, and I pretended being honest wasn't exactly what my thickheadedness needed.

His eyes demanded my attention. The green appearing nearly black beckoned me closer. He licked his lips, and I couldn't look away even if that was my only want. I knew that the more I looked, the more addicted he'd make me, and being addicted to him would end with me running. Because he didn't want commitment, and I didn't believe in love.

Right?

He made me feel things, and like a broken record, feelings were bad. If anything, it went against every rule we were taught in the Cupid handbook. Yet, here I stood. Him not knowing personal space, leaving no room between us, boxing me in like a feral animal, forcing me see his side of things.

No amount of pretending could deny the way he studied me as if I were the answers to all his problems.

We were fire and ice. He melted my frosted walls, and I gave him the cold shoulder as soon as he got nearer. He never seemed to get the memo, pushing until he obliterated them. No matter how tiring it was, I admired him.

"Why do you always run away from me?" he hostilely rasped, curiosity fighting with his temper. "Whether it's at Vex's, the club, or in the middle of a fucking forest, you always run." I didn't get a word in before he exhaled once more, "I'm so fucking sick of you running."

No pet, no Cupid, nothing but the cold truth.

"I'm not running," I lied, trying to sound unaffected, even as an indescribable ache festered inside. "I just don't want to be around you."

He chuckled, deep and gratingly. Anger sliced through me, but it wasn't really anger, but rather, disappointment—disappointment in myself for being so difficult.

"You are running. You always fucking run. No matter how close we get to real emotions, you turn the other way and act as if I mean nothing to you."

His features softened, the heat that was there now hidden beneath the sadness he offered me. This was his truth. His jaw ticked as he stared into my eyes, and I tried everything to look away, but his palm on my face held me there, and something in his eyes told me he was going to kiss me even if I didn't want him to. But that was a lie I couldn't believe myself, every morsel of my being wanted him to.

"Stop," I pleaded. I didn't know if I begged for him to stop, or to keep going, but his eyes didn't shy away from my lips as his mouth hovered over my own.

"Don't tell me to stop if you don't mean it. Use your safe word if it's too much."

"We can't do this," I tried again. "We can't be anything. I-I don't want you." The tremble in my voice was a dead giveaway. And he didn't take the bait.

"Again with the lies, Cupid. You can't lie to me." He stroked my bottom lip with his thumb, the caress gentle but probing. "If you truly want me to stop, use your safe word." His words were a challenge, he wanted me to prove myself to be a liar.

But I didn't want him, even if my treacherous body did.

"Say it, and I'll walk away. Say it, and I'll pretend we never met," he promised. "Say it, and you can move on without me."

Fear consumed me at the prospect of him walking away, of never seeing him taunt me again. Pain stabbed at me, imagining him with someone who wasn't me. I swallowed the choking feeling engulfing me. I couldn't say it. I couldn't tell him that it wasn't real—that I didn't want this—and I sure as hell didn't want him to walk away. Whether this hurt me in the end or not, I couldn't live another moment without knowing what he tasted like... at least once.

"No." The word sounded foreign on my tongue, almost like I went against my very nature saying it.

Pyro wasn't like me, he didn't pause, overthink, or even lack conviction. He knew what he wanted, always. That alone terrified me.

He didn't take any time before gripping my throat, closing the distance between us. We were all teeth and lips, tasting each other in a starved fashion. Just the fervor building between us melted the icy cold tendrils I wrapped around myself. They dissipated as his lips pressed against mine.

Cinnamon filled me as I licked the seam of my lips, stealing all the noises I made. A groan escaped me as I allowed him access, unable stop the way I fell apart at the seams.

We were the elastic band, together, and he had finally tugged too hard, too roughly. My hands snuck up his shirt even though I knew he didn't like to be touched until I earned it, but he didn't bat my hands away.

He pressed into me, urging me on, and a groan wretched from him as my fingers traced his chest, going to his jaw. I tugged on his perfectly gelled hair, bringing us closer, and I wanted this more than I wanted anything. There was not a single thing that mattered more at this moment than his lips against mine.

It was a religious experience, our aggressive movements and hip bucking while his tongue flicked inside my mouth, tasting exactly how I thought he would. Cinnamon, spiciness, and hedonistic pleasure.

He growled as my tongue traced his, teasing, wanting to feel what his felt like too. The rumble from his chest pressed against me, vibrating across my skin. Goosebumps lined my arms and neck, winding me up once more.

As if he couldn't help himself, he lifted me, gripping my thighs as I wrapped my legs around him. Our bodies rutted, clothed and guarded, but that didn't stop his grinding. It was too much, wanting more than what we could do in a storage room at a random-ass store.

I knew if we gave in to this, I'd be the one to fall apart, and the pieces of me would scatter at his feet.

And then what? He'd leave.

I wanted him to want me, forever. Not a moment, not a fuck in the dead of night. Something permanent and real.

Would he want it too?

Was I worth that kind of dedication?

His teeth dug into my bottom lip as my focus came back to our moving bodies. I wanted him to take off my clothes and push into me with abandon. Tear me apart, and then put me back together.

I wanted him to tell me that I was good and worthy of something I didn't believe in. That I was his, and only his. I wanted him to touch me everywhere and not leave a space of my body untouched.

Would he do that? Would he tell me that my needs were dumb—that I was some stupid Cupid who couldn't stop myself from ignoring what was right in front of my face?

Or would he ignore it just like I did, and tell me I was so good for him and that he wanted every part of me that I was willing to give him?

CHAPTER FIFTEEN

PYRO

Thinking Out Loud - Ed Sheeran

This is what I wanted, his freedom, his *everything*. His mouth pressed against mine, demanding, frantic, and unlike his worries, running wasn't my thing.

He grunted, threading his fingers through my hair. The pleasure his touch brought erased the near year we were apart.

It made it all worth it as he tightened his legs around me. Even with his forced vitriol, he fell apart for me.

Denying the body its needs always ended with an explosion, and this was ours. He tasted of strawberries and fear, a potent mixture worth absorbing.

My hips bucked toward him, wanting to erase the fabric keeping me from my goal. Once this heated moment passed, reality would rain hell on us both and he'd hide.

If I wanted it to last, I'd have to make it so.

Pulling away, I groaned at the loss of his warmth, wanting to coax his thighs around me once more, just to feel his erection and desperation.

"Unbuckle your pants," I directed, noting his kiss-swollen lips and disheveled appearance. It never escaped me how sexy this man was.

He didn't even stroke his own ego about his looks, and he could. Maybe that was half of the appeal. He existed for my praise rather than living within his own cockiness.

"W-what?" he hummed, his eyes not even opened as reality flashed back at him. His chest heaved with each breath, his palms flattening against the wall.

Did the cool temper him like it did me?

"Your pants," I said again, reaching for his belt. With a tug, his gaze landed on me. Understanding reflected there as his fingers went to work.

His rings were distracting today, every digit adorned with metal, covering the tattoos there. I didn't know which I liked more, the ink or the indentations I know he'd leave across my skin with his grip.

Once his belt was undone, he took no time to unbutton and unzip his pants. "Take out your cock." My instructions were clear, but his body shuddered with the defiance he always had. Most people didn't appreciate a fight during a scene, but with Valentine, I let it slide.

His cock came into view, each piercing glinting in the low light of the room. My mouth watered, craving his taste. While I stared openly, his eyes appreciated me slowly.

Leaning forward, I crouched, spitting on him. He groaned as his ring-covered fingers spread my saliva across his length.

"Stroke it for me."

He jolted when he made the first pass, his eyes fluttering as he bit his lip. "Fuck."

"Shh," I whispered, knowing we weren't glamoured anymore. Not that I ever needed him to hold my hand, because dragons had glamouring capabilities too. I didn't need him to know that tidbit, though. "Wouldn't want some poor store clerk catching you with your cock out, now would you?" My words were teasing with a little bit of fire. I couldn't resist running a finger over his shirt-clad chest. I wanted him bare, completely naked for my greedy perusal.

"Please, Pyro, it's been too long," he groaned as his hand made another slow pass. He wasn't stroking hard enough, avoiding his impending orgasm.

Leaning toward him, my head pressed against his. Gripping the front of his shirt, I tugged his lips to mine, needing to taste his moans as he released them.

He whimpered and I growled, putting all my weight against the wall. The chorus of our sounds sent shock waves to my balls, and it took all my self-control to hold back from whipping my own dick out and rubbing it against his. "Come for me, pet. Give me your truth."

With my words, he bucked against me twice more, and I took his mouth, consuming the little sounds he made as he squirted across his hand and my shirt.

"Such a good boy, coming for me without a single argument."

His sedated gaze met mine, no anger there, but so much yearning. I understood that expression. Too fucking well.

"Is someone back here?" an older voice sounded out nearby. Without thinking twice, I covered Val's mouth with my hand and glamoured us both.

So much for that secret.

Shock raised his eyebrows. Where that softness existed, trepidation followed. We scooted away from the searching person, a flashlight in their hand as they peered around all the boxes. Their boots echoed in the dark room as they went through the maze of storage. We wouldn't be seen, but the jizz droplets Val left behind wouldn't magically disappear as well.

We rushed out of the store, and against all odds, he didn't run from me. His eyes devoured me and I wasn't sure if it was the residual aftershock of lust or if he truly wanted more.

Either way, we headed toward the only hotel in town. I wasn't inept, I researched the Cupids' library. Their basic rules involved getting the most people in love to keep the Fates happy with balance.

By doing so, they were given *charges*; these people were destined to be together. Only one of the names and information was given, and the Cupids had to play it by ear and figure out the rest.

The fact that Valentine was the highest-ranking Cupid told me his dedication bordered on obsession.

No matter how good people were at their job, that alone could only get you so far. You truly needed complete dedication to have the numbers he garnered.

"We should go back," Valentine broke the rampant thoughts filling me. He didn't look at me this time and it gave me the answer from earlier.

His post-lust haze wore off, bringing him to reality and back to pretending to hate me. "We can tomorrow," I argued, thinking of how late it was here.

He shook his head. "That'll put me behind. We needed to at least get her normal schedule."

"She definitely doesn't do much. She works daily. If there's a person meant to be hers who's not only nearby but destined to arrive at some point, it won't be tonight."

"You don't know that," he grumbled, shaking his head. We made it to the hotel, the chime above the door sounding out as we walked in.

"Hello there," the person behind the counter announced, loudly chewing gum as they stared at their phone. Upon closer research, they were reading. Their eyes traveled over the words, still not looking up at us.

"How many?"

"Two," I answered.

"That's unfortunate," they responded. We only have one room.

"It's basically a graveyard here," Val moped, his voice bordering on petulant. Finally the clerk peered upward with a raised eyebrow.

"I said one room. One bed, too." Their eyes narrowed on us. "Are y'all from a convention or something."

"Or something," Val bitterly muttered.

They rolled their eyes dramatically, giving us a key. Not like a digital one either, a physical metal one we'd have to put in a deadbolt.

Handing them my credit card, I waited for them to give another salty remark. But instead of being rude, they quickly ushered us away, and I knew their e-book was the only reason.

We walked away, peering at the mini map offered at the entrance. We were in a dinky little motel and there were only six rooms. Walking east, we reached the third door easily.

"At least their books have more romance than what Cupids offer," Val muttered, not loudly, almost like his errant thought seeped through.

"You don't believe in love?" I questioned, knowing the answer already. It wasn't like people believed what they did as work.

Arson struggled with believing that Santa mattered because he only witnessed the back end of it. He saw the ins and outs, not experiencing the hopes and wishes kids had daily.

That was one of the reasons I wanted him to read the letters we received. They wrote to *him*. To tell him he changed their lives, gave them hope, and made them want to be better.

With Val, he didn't see love on the outside of his touch.

He only witnessed the back end.

"Love is like a disease. Everyone gets one at least once in their lifetime, but the cure is simply ridding yourself of it."

"Harsh."

His eyes connected with mine, wariness there. "If love is real, like an actual fucking thing, then why do only the people we give it to succeed?"

"What do you mean?" We entered the shabby place. At least the linens seemed clean. The walls were an off-white, and not because of the paint choice. More of a sun-bleached white from age and wear.

He wandered off to an ugly striped chair that had seen better days, sitting with a huff. "People divorce, a lot. The rates are high, and heartbreak is rampant."

"Okay?" I didn't know how to respond to that. Shit happened. Humans and monsters alike. Things out of the control of everyone occurred.

"If love was real, we wouldn't battle with a hate scale, either."

"Love and hate are lovers," I said. "You can't truly hate someone without actually experiencing some type of love."

"People hate others all the time," he argued.

"They think they do," I countered, invading his space. "They think they hate because they're confused and overwhelmed." I thought of him, how he said he hated me. Too often for my liking. But that didn't really mean what he thought.

Hate wasn't the way I forced his feelings to the surface. Instead, hate was the rules forbidding his entire desire for love.

He thought he didn't want love and didn't believe in it, but he did. The unfairness of him being warned away from it garnered his true ire.

The way he wanted to fall apart and allow me passage to his heart was obvious, and the more he feared the possibilities, the more he believed it was hate.

"You're unbearable," he replied, his words not minced or chopped, just cruel. I sidled up to him, even closer, needing him to see me.

"One day, when your stubborn ass has some clarity, you'll remember this moment. Then you'll fall to your knees and worship my cock, for being so wise."

His eyebrow rose, the harshness still there, hiding away his softer side. "You're the only one who has fallen to your knees, Jolly Boy. How does it look from down there?"

Humor curled my lip as I bit the inside of my cheek. "Looked like submission to me."

He didn't argue but we both knew he lost the argument. Regardless of whether I was above or below him, he fell apart *for* me.

LAUGH
BEST DAY
LOVE YOU
CARE 4 U
SWEET TALK
MISS ME
FRIEND ME
I ♥ YOU

CHAPTER SIXTEEN

VALENTINE

Wrecking Ball - Midnight String Quartet

The first assignment went without a hitch, the second too. Even if there was that singular moment in the store's back area.

It wasn't until the third where we didn't see eye to eye. "That's not how it works," I complained as Pyro watched the couple.

"They seem to be all wrong for each other," he suggested, his glasses—which I didn't know he wore—sat low on the bridge of his nose.

"Not all couples get along right away," I muttered, thinking of how we almost never did. Not that we were a couple, but same goes.

When I glanced back up, looking away from the sheet of details about the two we were helping, I noticed Pyro was gone from my view.

Where the hell did he go?

"Pyro," I lowly hissed, wondering if he hid behind a tree or something. We were seated in a park. About ten feet away, our charges argued, their hands flying with passion.

There was a man near them, tall, black hair, and in a suit. Immediately, without question, I knew it was Pyro.

He spoke to the guy and the couple's passionate hand waving stopped. This was wrong. We were meant to be unnoticed, not fucking talking to them. Shit.

The man threw his hands up in the air, anger his only reaction. The woman stomped off as well, and I wondered what Pyro said.

I stayed glamoured, sucking in my annoyance as I walked to him.

Even in his weirdly human form, he took my fucking breath away. No matter his shape or appearance, my eyes drew to him incessantly, like any electric current to a conductor.

"What the hell are you doing?" I hissed, the demand crueler than I meant for it to be. His eyes raked down my frame studiously, his glasses still hanging low on his nose. He reminded me of a librarian or some shit, attractive and intelligent, and why was my dick getting hard?

"Fixing it."

"Fixing?" My voice rose with the word, sucking my lungs free of oxygen.

"Yeah, I told him that if he didn't get his shit together, she'd find someone with a bigger dick to do it for him. He didn't like that—"

"Of course he fucking didn't! We don't talk to charges!" I yelled, anger my only emotions aside from concern for the results. "Xó is going to flip her shit."

His brow furrowed. "I don't see the issue, I don't have your love dust or whatever she called it. I had to do it the *old-fashioned way.*"

With a shake of my head, I flipped him off. "You know nothing about love."

He laughed, tipping his head back, and shit, my mind got stuck on how it sounded leaving his throat.

"I know that no person should treat another like a second choice to anything." His argument had validity, but we didn't choose. The Fates did.

We only pushed them together at their scheduled time.

"We do our job. That's it. Then we leave. We've already been here for too long."

"Well, I don't think they're going to work out," he trailed off, his eyes darting toward their retreated and separate forms.

"We don't go against fate," I groaned, struggling with words. Closing my eyes, portal-jumping to the Love Hub, leaving his sorry ass to find his way back home.

As soon as I got back, Paloma tapped her red-painted nails on my desk, as if waiting. "What they hell are you two doing?" Her voice was even, not too high, not too strained. She pointed to the love-hate scale with concern. It was like she didn't want to blow up without confirmation, and I respected that a hell of a lot.

"He fucked up, not me." I shrugged off the tension reflected on her forehead.

She shook her head, her eyes filled to the brim with aggravation. "You've never disobeyed a ruling."

"And I didn't," I let out, sighing loudly. "Pyro made his own rules."

"Why, why the hell would he do that?"

"He thought the old-fashioned way meant telling them they were shit for each other."

Her eyes nearly bugged out, and the way I laughed didn't help the seething glare she gave me. "You're going to fix this," she stated, pointing a finger at my chest. Her face didn't soften, if anything, it hardened as she stalked away. "And get him some love magic!"

She always yelled while walking away, and the annoyance I thought would leave me only multiplied because as she left, Pyro strutted in smugly.

Back in his normal appearance, his lips tilted with amusement, and my anger got the better of me. "My office."

"You have an office?" he taunted. "Ooh, I'm in trouble." My body heated at his words, wanting to stab him with my ballpoint pen.

He followed me as I guided him there. Yes, I had an office, but no, I didn't actually use it. Something about having a door separated from the rest was too weird, so I had them keep my old desk along with my office.

The door always stayed shut, and opening it for the first time in years had my eyes twitching. Inside, it stayed clean. Even the night crew knew it was unused but made sure dust didn't overtake every surface.

"You're such an ass," I grumbled as the door shut behind Pyro. His face still showed amusement, and I wanted to punch him.

"You don't seem to complain about my ass on any given day," he rebutted. He leaned against the door, his arm above his head with a nonchalant confidence settling around him.

"You're incorrigible," I hissed, getting closer to him.

"Yet, you still want to fuck me." He was so goddamn pretentious, but he wasn't wrong, and that was more infuriating than admitting it out loud.

A heavy exhale left me, my shoulders tight, and my pants even tighter. "It's the week of Valentine's now. There are rules and we're already falling behind." I ran a hand through my curls and tugged, needing a semblance of normalcy.

"Omi wants to give you love magic, I suggest you speak with her and figure it out."

"Is that why you brought me in here?" He pushed off the door, eating away the three steps between us. His eyes zeroed in on my lips. "You could've said this without a closed door."

The words were poignant, digging at me, seeking a reaction. His shoes touched mine, the loafers he rocked looking out of place against my studded boots.

"Y-yeah," I muttered, my collar feeling far too fucking tight. I hadn't looked upward, avoiding his penetrating gaze. He didn't allow that to halt his questions—he never did.

"For someone who uses lies as their crutch, you're really terrible at it."

"Fuck off," I groaned, but he held my jaw steady, not allowing me an escape. "I have work to do."

"Then by all means, Cupid. Do it."

I swallowed, my throat suddenly drier than the desert we left Ruby in. I walked backward, going to my desk. This was a bad fucking idea, and the heat in his eyes told me as much.

"I don't have—"

"Sit down, pet. Do I need to bribe you with some conversation hearts?"

"You're such a dick," I muttered, finally sitting in my chair. My breaths came out in pants, loud, erratic, and so fucking breathy, he had to know how he affected me.

Reaching into his breast pocket, he brought out an actual box of conversation hearts, and it took a lot for me to not laugh at his antics.

With all the smugness a person could offer, he strutted toward me, sitting on my desk in front of my chair. Setting down the box of candy, he waited for my eyes to meet his.

"Good boys are rewarded, remember?"

"What does that have—"

He quirked one eyebrow and waited for my answer. When he was in the mood for submission, deflection didn't work for him.

"Yes," I responded. He pulled out a little heart with the words *bite me* in the center. Waggling his finger at me, I leaned forward, putting my weight on the chair's armrests.

"Tongue," he commanded, and I stuck mine out. Without a warning, he placed the heart in his mouth, leaning forward just to insert it onto my tongue. He licked slowly, teasingly, and then as soon as he started, he stopped. "Eat."

I sucked on it for all of five seconds before crunching it with my molars.

His lips tilted and humor met my gaze.

"Such a good boy," he praised, running a hand through my curls. The way my body melted with the touch wasn't unexpected, each stroke of his fingers sent shivers down my spine.

MAEVE BLACK

CHAPTER SEVENTEEN
PYRO

Sensualidad - Bad Bunny, Prince Royce, J Balvin, Mambo Kingz, DJ Luian

He waited for my guidance, any sliver of direction. His head alternated with my fingers, as if he sought more than I offered, but would settle with scraps.

"So greedy," I mused, thinking of how he settled with my touch. "Was exhibitionism on your list?"

His head snapped up, immediate arousal dilating his pupils, making the blackness overtake the coral color.

"Use your words."

His cheeks flushed, the color deepening his already red cheeks. "The thought of getting caught has always…"

"Turned you on," I prodded.

"Yes, that."

Ah, the shame trailed down Val's throat, along his collarbones, before disappearing beneath his shirt. Moving my legs wider, I leaned backward, leaning on my elbows.

"Unzip me."

Immediately, he licked his lips. His hands shook as they reached for the button of my slacks. "Shit, I've never been this nervous."

Offering a sly grin, I waited for him to reach my waist. When he finally did, he let out a sigh. My cock strained against my pants, the tightness would be comical if the sweltering heat in Val's eyes didn't unravel me.

"It's taking a lot of control to not say fuck the slow play time and instead bend you over your desk to take what I want."

He visibly shuddered, his jaw ticking with concentration. "Whatever you want, I'll happily give."

"Good," I praised once more, grabbing another candy to place in his mouth. This time I didn't use my own for it. From the looks of it, he was too close to the edge for more teasing.

When he undid my slacks, he teased the band of my boxer briefs. "Can I?" I wanted to tell him how good he was for asking. Not touching me made him wild with want and that was why I usually kept him from doing so.

I nodded reassuringly, noticing the visible strain in his jeans. "You can't resist getting hard, can you?" It was a slight taunt, but the redder his face got, the more it told me he enjoyed it.

"I can't help what you do to me."

"Don't hold back," I rasped. Nervously, his hand pulled me from my confines, and a little hiss escaped him.

"Now, I want you to call Paloma for me."

"I-I," he stuttered, his eyes searching my own.

"While I apologize to her for not following the rules, you're going to take my cock down your throat." His teeth dragged across his bottom lip, alternating between nervous and hungry. "If you make me come while she's still on the phone, I'll reward you. If you're unsuccessful, I'll punish you."

He seemed to ponder the prospects of both. Whichever he decided, he was on a mission. Lifting the landline, he dialed the extension to Paloma, wasting no time to suck me down. I jolted at the action. He didn't hold back, his mouth working me over with precise movements, his piercings rubbing roughly against me.

"Yes?"

"Hello, Paloma," I answered, trying to keep the strain from my voice. Val fisted me, rotating with each of his bobs. I little groan attempted to escape me but I swallowed it down.

"Pyro," she responded with a lighter tone. "I'm guessing Valentine spoke with you." With the mention of his name, he sucked me harder, deeper, as if he wanted me to pay attention to only him and not the woman on the other side of the phone.

When his second hand gripped my balls, tugging on them, I had to bite back the hiss that wanted to escape. Pleasure zipped through me, tingling from my toes to my groin, promising release. Pulling back, he teased the head of my cock with the barbells, his eyes watching mine with promise.

"He did," I barely uttered, the tightness drawing up. For this moment, I was his puppet, my strings tugged and pulled in support of him. "I wanted to apologize."

My body shuddered as Val's mouth traveled south, licking every inch of available skin. Without asking for direction, he wet his fingers and teased my hole.

The foreign feeling had me jolting with shock, but I didn't reprimand him, I just ran my fingers through his curls and shoved my cock deeper, punishing him with a steady punch of my hips.

"Oh, no need. You're new and will learn."

"Regardless, I know it's not easy losing someone as amazing as Xó during the rush..." I trailed off, barely biting back the pleasure-filled groan as Val entered me and deep-throated me at the same time. "So, I apologize. Val told me I'm due for some love magic?"

"Yes, he's correct. We'll be able to help you and maybe you can knock him down a few pegs."

With that, Val took no prisoners. He pressed against that rough spot inside me, sucking me down with loud slurps. I gasped out and felt my ass clench around him.

He kept his pace and I fell apart, spurting my release down his throat. Before letting out all the noises building up, I clicked Mute, and used his head as my personal fuck toy, knowing my well-spent dick would appreciate a break.

"You did such a good job, pet. Do you know that?"

"You taste like cinnamon sticks," he rasped, his dick-swollen lips all puffy and perfect. I've had my cum compared to hot tamales, so cinnamon sticks was a new one. Spicy, with enough kick, but not too overwhelming.

He eyed the phone and then glanced back at me. Paloma spoke about how the love magic would work, that it'd be fairly simple. Whatever she said went through one ear and out the other. My only focus becoming the man in front of me, panting and red-faced. We were still on the call, even if muted. Covering his face was a layer of sweat, trailing down his temples and dampening his curls.

"I'm going to take care of you now, okay?"

He nodded, and I unmuted the call. "I'll be down in twenty, if that's all right with you?" She seemed to contemplate her choice but confirmed and hung up.

"How would you like to come?" I asked Val, allowing him to choose for once. His eyes flashed with desire, one I recognized similar to my own.

There was truly nothing off-limits for me at this point. Whatever he wanted, I'd give. He earned it. He traced his bottom lip with his tongue, his thoughts louder with each exhale.

"I want to feel you," he gritted out, worry meeting me. His eyes danced over my face, waiting for a reaction. I wasn't lying to myself when we were at Vex's and the thought of him inside me appealed to me.

It did.

Standing up, I wordlessly took off my cuff links. Our eyes never left one another's as I removed my vest, then my shirt. He panted, his chest rising and falling in rapid succession. It was like he couldn't sit any longer, coming toward me, helping with the entire removal of my shirt. It slid down my shoulders and his grip appeared firm and sure.

He raked his fingers through my hair, pulling backward. The little action stole a smile from me. "You'll tell me if you hate it?"

I swiftly nodded, knowing anything he did would turn me on. There wasn't a brain cell left for any type of doubt.

Silently, he reached for my throat, peppering kisses across the flesh there. He sucked on my Adam's apple, his tongue laving before he bit down. A hiss was his only response.

He was a greedy man, his hands sliding up my waist, digging into each ridge across my stomach. Not stopping until he reached my nipples, he twisted, eliciting a rumble.

Against my skin, he smiled, laying little kisses over each bite as his teeth dug into me. I didn't stop him, allowing him every ounce of exploration. It didn't take a genius to know Paloma expected us soon, but there were no fucks to offer.

This moment was ours. One where only we existed and the rest was fodder.

In a swift move, he unclasped my pants, letting them pool at my feet as his mouth latched onto the pebbled flesh of my nipple. He groaned when my hand snaked into his hair, pressing him against my chest, rubbing his face against my damp skin.

Warmth diluted to a simmer as my body shuddered with pleasure. He was a toucher, someone who took the majority of their time tracing every inch of their lover.

Being under the hands of that was more than pleasant, and I couldn't say I wanted it to end. Never had I been a liar, and I wouldn't start now.

"You taste so good to me," Valentine whined, his voice throaty and ravenous. He nipped at my ribs, trailing his ring-clad hands across my flank.

When pressure met the muscles of my back, I just knew he'd bruise me. He pressed harder when sweet sounds left me.

"That's right, pet. Just like that," I encouraged as his rings dug into me. A bite of pain sliced through me as his grip grew harsher. "Fuck, you're good at this."

He hummed, releasing little pleased sounds as he raked his teeth down my chest. Sliding back up with as much hunger, he finally gripped my erection.

The hardness surprised me, it felt near combustion. Usually, control came easy, something I trained myself to have, but as he took his time, and I felt weak beneath his touch.

"I love how turned out you look right now, the ruddy cheeks and glazed look," I complimented him, noting his pupils were blown out. His hand lazily stroked at my length, his mouth not leaving my hips, sucking feverishly.

"I'm nervous," he admitted, laying a kiss on my pubis. I lowered to his level, craning his head upward.

"Let me guide you." Relief softened his shoulders as he nodded. "On your back," I directed, and he fell with a thud. A chuckle escaped us both as the noise came out far louder than expected. I leaned over him sucking him, making sure to pay attention to every piece of metal, teasing while drooling across his length. He stretched me a little earlier with his fingers, and it'd have to be enough when we were lacking lube.

I climbed over him, lining up with his cock. His eyes didn't leave where I hovered. Sliding down, his chest moved with harsh pants.

"Fuck, you're so tight," he groaned from beneath me, his words more a garble than not. My body relaxed as I finally seated myself on him. The way his piercings pressed inside me, holding perfectly against that sweet spot inside had black spots coating my vision.

"How does it feel, pet?" I asked him, his entire body shuddering, and I hadn't even begun to move. He blinked slowly, in a daze.

"So good," he groaned. I slid up on him and his body bowed with me, chasing the movement. "Shit, shit, don't move." The whimper encouraged me, and I lifted again. "Stop, please, Pyro. I'm too close. You're so fucking tight."

Warmth pooled in my stomach as my own ache built up. My once softened length stood straight, craving friction.

"Think Paloma will come searching for us?" I teased, rising and falling several times while Valentine pressed into my flesh so roughly it throbbed. My entire body feel stretched to its limit, a feeling I never experienced before. "See you whimpering on the floor, deep inside me?"

My feelings for this man expanded with my chest, inflating as my heart hammered, telling me that this couldn't be all we had. It wasn't enough. His attempt at keeping me still didn't work, but the pleasant pain it came with was worth it.

I took my pleasure from him, riding him with undulated thrusts. He cried out, craning his head back in passion. Leaning forward, I latched onto his pulse point. The salivating came back, leaking as my incisors fought to expand. It took me clamping my mouth shut, pulling away, to keep the natural feeling from taking over.

"I'm going to come," he rasped, perspiration coating his skin. I licked the little droplets gathering on his chest.

"What are you waiting for, baby," I hissed, noting my slip of the endearment. His eyes hit mine and he pulsed inside me, gripping my hips as he shook. Not stopping my movements, I coaxed each spurt. "That's it," I said, gripping my own length, thrusting as my body pulsed with tendrils of electricity. The burn overwhelmed me and my wings flourished, spreading wide as I grunted through my release.

Val whimpered as he softened inside me, but my cock kept leaking, each beat of my heart releasing a new stream. I don't think I ever came this hard in my life. By the time I softened, the tugging became too much.

His entire chest was covered with my release, ropes of white against his ruddy skin. Even his face had a few drops and the sex-dazed expression reflected at me was worth every moment.

Above his head, he rested his arms, and I stared at the tattoos mostly hidden. Tentatively, I traced them, dragging my finger over every inked inch, wanting to paint them to memory.

When his soft snores reached my ears, I slowly rose off of him. Using what magic Santanas had, I got a rag and cleaned him up. His sedated expression soothed a part of me.

And for the first time since the night we met, I held him, telling his sleeping form how amazing he was and that I wasn't going anywhere.

MAEVE BLACK

CHAPTER EIGHTEEN

VALENTINE

Pointless - Lewis Capaldi

Pyro tried cornering me every moment since our excursion in my office. I heard him when my body was mostly asleep.

I'm not going anywhere.

But I would. We both knew it. He fell asleep, his arms and legs tangled around me. Before he could stir, I stood, got dressed, and wondered when I'd stop running from him and our reality.

My heart physically felt fine, but inside? It ached. A pinch so agitating that it constantly reminded me of how bad I was.

Lovesick.

I'd heard about this from other Cupids. It was where a person denied their feelings so much—directly hurting themselves from the tether being tugged on too much. Whatever that meant for us scared me.

We didn't make sense.

It felt different in my office. Our bodies pressed together, the soft way he topped me, giving me my orgasm by taking it from my limbless body. He coached me, talking me through how to fuck him. He wrecked me and I was still there in a state of unrest.

Since our moment with me expertly fucking up again, I had evaded his every advance. In return, he outranked me in the office. He got the love magic imbued, and his name toppled mine on the chart. It was a show of power, a silent *fuck you* to my immaturity.

The day I noticed was the day his perfectly planned-out unraveling-of-Valentine began.

His eyes followed me as I rushed away from the main room. He sat, his legs widened with confidence, a smirk my only warning.

Everyone gathered, talking about their Valentine's charges, how most were super sweet, buying flowers, chocolates, and rings. *Fucking rings.*

How could they be so committed to a person they only just met? Love didn't magically happen to anyone else. You didn't just wake up one day and find the love of your life, right?

Heading to my office—which has been my hiding place from Pyro because it has a lock—I noticed a heart-shaped box on my desk.

It was gaudy and red, velvet wrapped with a big-ass bow. My heart hammered. *Is this a joke?* Bile rose, love. What a stupid fucking concept.

"Knock, knock," Xóchi sounded out before opening my door. Her round belly and rosy cheeks welcomed me in kind.

"How's the baby?" I asked first, wanting to avoid the concerned gaze she carted. Her eyes darted to the red heart on my desk, and I knew she wouldn't be letting it go.

"Amazing, while I grew fast, they think I still have a good month to go."

"That's wild," I replied. "Normal gestation is nine months."

"For humans," she confirmed. "There's never been a Cupid-dragon."

"Is that what we're calling it?"

She tsked, walking toward me. "Not *it*. It's not a foreign creature."

"Isn't it, though?" I teased with a furrowed brow. She shook her head in amusement.

"You will forever be a pain in my ass, brother."

"Yeah, I know."

"You going to tell me why you've got Valentine's Day paraphernalia on your desk that you've never used?"

"Ugh," I gritted out. "Who knows. A prank, I'm guessing."

"Hmm," she hummed, curiosity far too potent for me. Her hands clasped over her stomach, rubbing circles. The way she naturally did it made me wonder if she even noticed.

"When are you finally going to admit what's going on with you and Pyro?" Swallowing the gravel lodged in my throat, I shook my head in indifference.

"There's nothing going on." *Lies.*

"You always struggled with emotions." She ignored my complete disregard for the truth. "When we were younger and you flirted with the Cupids in training, you pretended you didn't feel anything."

"I didn't," I rejected the idea. Always. She chuckled with mirth, humoring me.

"Okay, you 'didn't.'" She rolled her eyes, coming closer to me. She seemed in far less pain in the week or so she'd been gone. "However, it worsened when that one Cupid..." she trailed off, tapping her chin thoughtfully. "Azar, was it?"

Our gazes connected. I was sure she could sense my disbelief. "Whatever," I deflected.

"Azar stole your first kiss. Hades, all your valentine cards, chocolates, and especially the conversation hearts you loved so much."

I huffed out, trying to forget the boy who I grew up with turning into a ruthless teenager who tormented me. Every Valentine's Day, he'd ruin it.

Stomping on my little mailbox, eating my candy, and even going as far as writing hurtful notes on cards others gave me.

He would point at me in front of everyone and say I was a loser.

"Doesn't ring a bell," I rasped, emotion burning behind my eyes. That stupid kid turned into a big asshole too. He became a Cupid, and while he worked at this specific Love Hub—there was more than one—he took every moment to hurt me.

I'd get a charge, he'd rush to them behind my back.

I'd win a huge bonus, which only came with street cred, truly, and then he'd say he did it and gave me credit.

No matter how I succeeded, he was always there to rub it in my face.

"The way you're grinding your molars and fisting your palms tell me otherwise."

"Can we not?" I grumped, thinking of all the things in life I never gave time to. Not the pain, the hurt, or the fact that my parents not once noticed my bullied childhood.

It made sense how I threw away the only man who ever vied for my attention, working hard toward it, and never once giving up.

"We need to," she argued, her hands gripping both my arms. My sister was quite a bit smaller than me, all of my sisters were, in fact. Well, Dion was tall as hell, but still a half head beneath me. "You're my brother, Val. My best friend in the whole wide universe." Tears burned my eyes as heat bloomed across my skin. Out of all the family I had, Xóchi never shied from affection, even if it made me uncomfortable.

Unless it was Pyro.

Her eyes bore into my own, forcing my train of thought away from the beast who owned me. "You deserve love, brother."

"It's not real," I automatically responded. It was the same answer I always had, the one that acted almost like a defense mechanism.

She shook her head with a sigh. "You can't look at me and Arson and tell us what we have isn't real."

My heart panged with her words. They had love. But it was a fluke. They were special somehow. I swore it.

"That's different."

"It's not," she immediately challenged, cupping my face next. "You're worthy of love, the best kind in the world. You're even worth cheesy Valentine's gifts, and love songs, but especially the chalk candy you call delicious."

I sputtered out a laugh, thinking of how everyone bagged on the crunchy hearts but never gave them a real chance.

Peeps? Those were gross. Conversation hearts, though? They were delicious as fuck. I'd always loved them and Red Hots. Knowing how Pyro tasted only further confirmed my addiction to the flavor.

"They're goddess tier, Xó." I narrowed my eyes at her until she giggled. She shuffled around my desk, sitting on my big chair. It made her seem even smaller as she let out a sigh, raising her feet.

"They're not, but I'll let it slide."

While I went to grab a drink, the sound of a seal breaking tore my attention away. Her eyes roamed the velvet heart, emotion welling in her eyes.

"What?"

"Nothing," she muttered with a lip wobble. "Nothing at all."

"Xóchi, what's wrong?" I asked again, wondering if she was in pain. Her eyes met mine, red-rimmed and already wet.

"He loves you, Val."

I shook my head. "Who?"

She slid the heart toward the edge of the desk and I made my way back over. Inside the box, where my sister broke the seal, sat a card.

> *Stubborn Brat,*
>
> *I'd call you Cupid, but it feels sort of redundant at this point.*
> *I know you hate the fourteenth, and I also know it's approaching quickly.*
> *But one thing I know you hide that you love is chocolate.*
> *Not that I notice everything you do.*
> *Like the conversation hearts you enjoy and the little*
> *red balls of bitterness that you seem to crunch when no one's watching.*
> *Enjoy these. I found them in this little shop*
> *while doing one of my assignments.*
> *There's even three cinnamon-infused ones.*
> *(And no, I didn't stuff my dick in it.)*
>
> *Forever yours,*
> *Jolly Boy*

Emotion threatened to take over, and I couldn't help but smile over his dick comment. I'm super grateful for Xó not mentioning it. We were close, but not *that* close.

"He just likes my tattoos," I offered, not wanting to admit the clamminess of my palms and the way my skin seemed to itch with discomfort.

"Yeah, okay," she mocked, giving me the wildest facial expressions. "Go out there and tell him you want him. Have his babies."

"Babies? At my ripe age, how about no?"

She chuckled, absentmindedly rubbing her stomach once more. "Maybe one day."

I nodded at her and immediately shook my head. She noticed too quickly and raised a single manicured eyebrow.

"While I love your visits, was there a specific reason you stopped by?"

A nod, a belly pat, another nod, and then a yawn. "Pyro's kicking your butt on the charts," she noted. "At first, I thought it was going to be a disaster. Omi contacted me and told me I set her up for failure, nearly putting me in labor, but then she called a couple days later with hope."

"He's a natural," I admitted, thinking about how he grasped knowledge quickly, constantly growing and adapting for what was needed. "He was made for it."

"He's struggling," she confessed, then placed a hand over her mouth. "That's not my secret to tell." The hurried way she tried erasing her words didn't placate me, it made me want to dig deeper.

"With what?" My mind went to worst-case scenarios. Starting with illness and ending with him leaving this place because of me.

While I avoided him at every turn, I didn't want him gone. No, I wanted him near, where I could stare at him with longing, all while avoiding giving myself the happiness I deserved.

"Ask him. If you care about him and his well-being, ask him."

With that, she rose, stretching with a little cat-like yawn. "Arson should be here, waiting for me. He won't let me realm travel and insists on carrying me everywhere."

"Well, he seems like a good enough man for you."

"He's better than good enough. He's the best man for me."

My lips curved with happiness, knowing my sister was content with her choices and with the man she loved brought me so much peace.

Rising onto her tiptoes, she kissed my cheek, embedding a bit of her love magic with the touch. "Be kind to yourself and know that even if you're a pain in the butt, you're worth every ounce of love Pyro has to offer." She started walking off before turning once more. "And you better earn his love too. We both know you're difficult when cornered, and he deserves to feel loved and wanted as well."

Love.

Wanted.

My stomach burned with disgust as I realized he tried to make me fall in love with him, he even went out of his way to tease me.

He deserved better.

I needed to be the better he deserved.

MAEVE BLACK

CHAPTER NINETEEN
PYRO

El Perdedor - Enrique Iglesias

He hid.

He ran.

He did everything but give in.

Day one, it was a note and a box of chocolates. Ones I knew he devoured. Ones I wished I could've fed him while massaging his body, whispering the sweet things I knew he needed to hear.

My body warred with my mind. My dick wanted inside him while my heart demanded him to see me. It wasn't a hard ask, just a fucking inch. Sure, I'd take the whole damn mile, but that inch was my in. I needed that *in*.

Day two, I snuck into his office while he helped another couple. I put rose petals all over, thinking of how much he hated the prospect of romance.

But I couldn't help the little part of me that was excited to show him I cared. I scattered a box of conversation hearts over the desk he sucked me off on, creating a big heart with an arrow.

I grabbed the box of valentine cards kids usually give to their classmates, making sure I got a cheesy one.

Humans are the worst, good thing we're monsters, it read, and I laughed, thinking of how Val hated everything and everyone, even sometimes me. Signing the card with the worst dragon drawing known to man, I left with hopes he wouldn't hate it. Or at the very least, that he knew I cared.

Because I did, and that wasn't changing.

When I left Val's office, I found my brother leaning against my desk, his hands in his pockets. "Pyro," he said with a wave of his hand.

He looked worse for wear, bags still nestled under his eyes, his skin a little less vibrant. "Arson."

It wasn't overtly friendly, but there was still that small part of me worrying at my insides, scraping for the only destiny written for me.

"Go for a walk?"

I eyed my desk, how there was not a single charge left for today. I had three for tomorrow and two for the day after, but I'd wrapped up five today, quickly.

Taking a page from the Valentine cheat book, I gave them their needs and went on my merry way. The only difference was the subtle things I did to force them together faster.

After the first botched attempt, I learned something valuable. You could absolutely think you hated someone, the passions burning like a wildfire in the dead summer, but in the end, the ones who challenged your entire existence were the ones worth knowing. They didn't settle for easy or the bare minimum, they hunted for the ball-squeezing, heart-stabbing, and raw kind of love.

"Yeah, I'm free." If Val was here, I'd watch him instead. He was my only obsession aside from making a name for myself.

We went down to the base area where the biggest portal resided, and within moments we were in front of a little house, not to unsimilar to my own. It was covered in snow—sweet, but practical—and it wasn't located within

Santa's workshop.

Pride swelled in my chest as realization hit. "You've done it," I whispered, awe laced in my words. A ringing hit my ears, matching my heartbeat exactly.

"She deserved a fresh start, our babies too."

Emotion gathered behind my eyes, reminding me that my brother wasn't a bad person. After years of me forcing him to exist within a cage I trapped him in, he finally accepted it.

I didn't have to follow that same path. Putting myself in a never-ending box of purpose only stopped me from being happy.

"What about home?"

Home.

Was it ever really a home or a prison where all the memories existed?

My home was Valentine in my arms snoring lightly as I traced his inked body with lazy movements.

"It's staying there, I even had them do renovations for the drakes. It's going to be a better place. One free of hatred."

"I don't know what to say," I choked out, clutching the back of my neck, warmth filling me.

"Give me ten years. Ten years to love what I do, and raise my kids within it. Let me relearn what it is to be a Santana and why it's a selfless act," he went off, tears dripping down his face. "Then the reins are all yours. I never meant to take your dream away, brother."

Our gazes clashed, too much left unspoken and yet everything said altogether. I nodded and he patted my back.

"I spoke to Mom and Dad," he admitted, his jaw tense with the words. "We're redefining the by-laws with conditions. We can't grow with the newer generations if we're stuck where we started."

My chest pinched with emotion as everything fell into place. He was giving me my dream back. Sure, it was doused with a bit of patience and the willingness to forgive, but most importantly, it coated me with hope.

"It's all I've known," I let out, a shaky cry escaping my lips as I fell to my knees. "When you decided to stay, a part of me broke." The admission felt like an excavation, taken from the deepest parts of my heart. "I've never felt so worthless."

"Don't say that," he retorted, agony in his pinched expression. "You were the backbone of this family. The strength and glue. If not for you, we'd have failed Earth eons ago."

I nodded but felt that pit of despair still resting above my lungs, making it hard to breathe. Honesty freed us all, and this was my truth.

"I love him," I panted, scratching at my chest as it beat faster. Maybe if I ripped through the skin, it'd stop aching. He hurt it by running, and I did what I did best.

Tried to fix it.

"I know."

Just two words, but they held more weight and acknowledgment than anything else. "I won't choose between him and being Santa. It'll always be him, Arson. He's it for me."

"Does he know this?" Shaking my head, I pressed my palms into my eyes, wanting nothing more than to sink the knowledge into Valentine's thick skull.

If he could only *see* me.

"He fights me at every turn, his fire so much brighter than my own."

"If anyone could convince him, it's you. I've never met a more determined person in my life. You don't give up easily."

I thought back to just yesterday, the way he constantly avoided me. It made me want to give up. If not for the stubborn way my heart claimed him, maybe I would have.

"I just want him to fall for me." I dwelled on my own thoughts, annotating them across my brain, giving me fuel to not crash and burn, taking him with me.

"Have you tried tying him down?"

His idea stole a laugh from deep within me and an idea formed. Vex's. That was our moment. I knew it in his posture, how he freely gave in to me. That was where he realized he did in fact feel something.

"No, but now that you mention it, I've got an idea." He gave me a two-finger salute, his wings expanding.

"I'm going to go spend time with my wife," he announced, tapping his chest. "She's in pain."

Hurt ebbed its way beneath my skin and into my veins. I wanted that connection, to sink my teeth into Valentine and feel what he felt so I could describe it to him.

Maybe then, he'd stop running away.

The next three days, I showered him with little tidbits. He couldn't ignore it anymore. Not with the little smiles he tried to hide and not with the way he rushed to his office every morning, waiting for his next surprise. He left every night with a softness he only offered me when at my mercy. It was my way of taking care of him.

Tomorrow was Valentine's Day, and today, I filled his office with *tithonia diversifolia,* a flower from his home. One that symbolized faith, loyalty, and adoration. The meaning wouldn't be lost on him, and it was the last day before my big surprise. The thing that would make him mine without argument.

When he sauntered into work today, there was almost a pep in his step, a little flush as he stopped at the door, the note beneath his fingertips.

He traced over it, no doubt reading my promises of devotion. I hid in plain sight, my body humming with the glamour around me.

Val rubbed his jaw, brushing his fingers through his hair with the tenderest smile. Would he be mine tomorrow?

Would he finally give in and say yes?

MAEVE BLACK

My Sweet Pet,

Today is an important day. Unlike last year, you're seemingly on the schedule.

But I intend to remedy any bad mood you have tonight.

You're mine. I can feel it in every breath you take when you think I'm not

watching. I see it in your little smirks and bright smiles.

Do you remember what I said when we first met? No? I'll remind you.

I don't need your life, pet. I need your freedom.

I've come to get my reward, because unlike you, I've been a really fucking good

boy. Waiting is no longer an option. The longer we're apart, the more my heart

beats its intentions against my ribs. I'm all yours, but will you be mine?

My Valentine?

All yours, forevermore.
Your Jolly Boy

CHAPTER TWENTY

VALENTINE

Like I'm Gonna Lose You - Meghan Trainor, John Legend

E very day since the box of chocolates, I've had little and big gifts waiting for me. Notes filled with promises I wanted him to keep. Where he asked me to be his. That today would be the day he intended to ask me.

Once again, my door had a note on it. This time it was in bright pink.

Too many things consumed me. The fact that he truly hadn't stopped trying to win me over. Even though he didn't need to. I was his. I had been since the moment I walked into that play party. But then, we had boundaries of sex and no emotions. We both set them. I didn't want that. Just thinking about the way we joined together the first time had my legs weak, but it also instilled trepidation.

That place both freed me and shackled me to my fears. It didn't offer peace or calmness anymore. When I thought of Vex's, I thought of how unsure I felt.

Opening my office door, my smile stayed plastered on my face. From floor to ceiling, my office was a bright marigold color. The sunflowers of my home on every surface. There was no way to tell for certain that he knew what this flower symbolized, but it healed a part of me that wasn't his to fix.

Letting out a contented sigh, I wondered where he'd be taking me. Would it be dinner, a dance place, maybe even the park would be an amazing place to get lost in his gaze.

Hope, the traitor, fueled me. This week had gone smoother after my conversation with my sister. She reassured me and reminded me how I didn't truly give Pyro a chance.

He deserved to have me limitlessly. I closed my eyes, imagining how I'd beg him to give me a chance. Maybe we could start from scratch?

The pitter-patter of my chest hit harder as I gave in to my own feelings. Was it love? Was that what this whole thing has been since day one?

Love at first sight happened to people in movies, books, and even anyone Cupids like me designated as such, but for me, someone who didn't get the magical touch?

Finally reaching my desk, I laid the newest note next to the others, grabbing a handful of conversation hearts out of the bowl I'd put the copious amounts he'd given me in.

"Delivery!" Paloma shouted, her voice sending in a tendril of disappointment. I figured he'd be hand-delivering my package today. Part of me hoped I'd be able to thank him... in person. Maybe even on my knees.

It'd been only days, but it was so long to my deprived soul.

The knock on my door didn't shock me. But when it was a random delivery person giving me an invisible package, I scrunched my face in confusion.

The person flickered away and as soon as they did, the glamour dropped, and along with it my entire mood. In my palms was a box.

A black box.

One that hit the most insecure part of me.

It was fairly similar to the one I received a year ago to the date.

No. I gripped it angrily, immediately being zapped with that familiar magic. This wasn't happening. He couldn't just expect me to go against every grain of my being for some non-emotional agreement. Not again.

Instead of allowing it to unwrap, dragging me into something I knew I couldn't handle, I made sure to walk outside of my office, walking directly toward the main trash can. He'd know he fucked up, right? This was answer enough... right? I held the ribbons, knowing they'd snap and unravel if I let them go. Not fucking happening.

His eyes focused on me, not even hiding his scrutiny. We were on a warpath with zero chance of survival. Would this denial be the final nail in the coffin? Would he give up, walk away, and simply not care anymore?

I didn't want that, yet I didn't address my own problems and talk them through with him. It irritated me how aware I was of my own issues and didn't fix them immediately. What was I thinking?

Making a show of it, I carelessly dropped it in the bin. His wings unfurled, bouncing outward with ferocious strength. Those scary, beautiful things forced other Cupids to move out of his path.

Shit.

Somehow, I knew this was going to happen, but I didn't stop my own stupidity. I turned toward my office, waiting for him to unleash everything.

We couldn't keep doing this. Passion was one thing, our push and pull, the need to run, and his chase.

It was wrong on so many levels and it had to end.

The door slammed behind me, the hinges crying out as it rattled the entire frame. Pyro seemed more monster than himself, standing there, commanding every ounce of my attention. His eyes glowed. Not the normal flicker of flames, no, they *burned*. Every inch of them was encased in fire, scorching me with vehemence. They licked his eyelids, catching his eyelashes, and somehow became brighter as he seethed.

His body, tense and formidable, didn't stop at the door, no, he charged toward me, smoke and ash leaving his nostrils and mouth.

Right now, his dragon was in control and not once had I heard about this or witnessed it firsthand. I didn't speak, knowing my pension for saying all the wrong things when it mattered most would only worsen the predicament I found myself in.

When he stood a foot from me, the steam billowed around me, wrapping me in an angered cocoon. Somehow, I knew he wouldn't hurt me. Not anything I wouldn't ask for or earned for in this constant battle I forced us into.

Nimble fingers reached for me, pressing against my sternum, forcing me to peer up at him. It wasn't quite hatred that painted his features, but something molten all the same.

"You push too much, Cupid." His words came out with fumes, an almost roar of hisses and growls. I scoffed, regretting it immediately. The petulance he stirred inside me ignited over the simplest things.

"You're too fucking bossy for a subordinate," I challenged. "I'm above your pay grade." Why did my mind go here? Why did I push and poke?

"You don't get paid," he argued, a haze leaving from the corner of his lips.

"Regardless," I uneasily responded with a swallow. The need to pause this situation, then go back and grab the box I tossed and apologize, had me falling to my knees. Xó's words echoed like a pendulum in my head. *You better earn his love too. We both know you're difficult when cornered, and he deserves to feel loved and wanted as well.*

His expression didn't falter, ever the dragon wanting to take his treasure back to a cave or whatever shit they did.

I hated that I didn't like what I did to him. He was all stiff composure and I was restless chaos. We didn't fit and he kept trying to connect our pieces, but mine were jagged where his were smooth. I was childish and broken and he was composed and complete.

A flash of something flickered momentarily. Just as soon as it appeared, it disappeared. I recognized that emotion well. *Hurt.*

"I'm sorry," I let out. Those words weren't offered easily. Not from me to others, it was worse than accepting love as a real thing. *I'm sorry* meant admitting I cared about him. *I'm sorry* defined the lines we crossed. *I'm sorry* wasn't enough.

He breathed heavily, his shoulders rising and falling while his wings beat angrily. There was a part of him that existed behind the wounded scowl, much like me. But the proprietary part facing me right now needed something. I wasn't sure what, but in good faith, I exposed my throat, dropping back onto my heels. Ever the submissive.

Here it felt natural, real, and not some contractual obligation that felt permanent. That was what a lack of communication offered, pain and resentment. Or in my case, anxiety.

A rumble that shook the entire room sounded out, the vibrations making me second-guess my vulnerable position.

But as I snuck a peek at him through my peripherals, I noted his agony. Behind the hatred, behind the anger, and even behind the annoyance, and the need to fuck me into submission, lived true heartbreak. The true kind that scarred, a constant webbing of never-quite-healed flesh.

"You make really stupid choices," he growled, enunciating the words like a whip against my sensitive skin. "You hurt me because you're hurt, Valentine." His voice broke with his words. "You don't let me in."

He crouched, his wings touching me for the first time ever. They fluttered, the claws at the end of each ridge scraped across me.

They carved with pain but offered a type of companionship I didn't deserve. He held back but his wings couldn't resist what they sought. Even with their harsh and contorted appearance, they were as tender as they could be given the circumstances.

My skin burned where they dragged, almost singeing my skin with their marks. His face hadn't calmed either, but he dragged his nose across my pulse point. The puffs of air against me both hot and promising. The pants scattered over me with purpose but also seared me with their claim.

"*Mine*." It was like the word was stripped from the deepest part of him. Feral and unseen. I did this. I tortured him with my back and forth.

He didn't deserve that.

No one did.

"Yours," I confirmed, allowing him to breathe against my throat with his claim.

His lips pressed against my flesh, hotter than coals and stinging with their distinct warpath. "You can't run anymore. I can't do this if you don't give me your promise." His words were so raw, like he stripped his entire soul to release them.

Like drinking cement, I swallowed sharply. "I'm not running anymore." Saying that might've been the hardest words to leave my mouth. "I'm tired of hurting us both."

His eyes flickered once more, a softness trying to drag through them. "Why did you throw away my gift?"

Biting my lip, I closed off my expression. "I didn't want to be a toy anymore."

He rumbled, ever the monster. "You were never a toy."

I shook my head in denial. "At Vex's, I was a toy. Our agreement was to fuck without attachments."

"That's what you wanted." Opening my eyes to his now black ones took my rebuttal away. I agreed to his terms, even laying my own out there.

"I don't want that anymore," I confessed, shivering at my own truth. He shook his head as if exasperated. His forehead wrinkled, forcing his eyes shut with the action.

"You have to be honest with me. That rule still fucking applies. No more walking around your feelings, no more lying about how I'm making you feel, and no more running."

"So demanding," I groaned, throwing my head back in exhaustion. He deserved the best version of me. "I promise."

"If you're scared, or feel unsafe, or you just need me to fuck you into the next damn century, just use your words."

His wings still traced me, the skin raw and broken in some places. It stung, but somehow soothed the rampant beating in my chest.

My knees ached as they dug into the wood floor. Almost dusting the area was a mixture of ash, charred shapes, and singed marks.

His hand, covered in black soot, gripped my jaw, tilting it. "We can take it slow."

"I don't want slow," I protested. "Just promise me it's permanent, that these feelings are real."

He tapped my chest, over the tattoo of a mangled heart being gripped by a skeletal fist and impaled with arrows. "This is real, baby. This is what love is. It's not easy or sensible. It ebbs and flows, and sometimes confuses the best of us. Love hurts and it heals, it steals and gives. If you let it, it'll be the most comforting experience in the world. But if you don't nurture it, taking advantage of its tenderness, it'll turn on you, betraying you in the same fashion you treat it."

"Fuck."

"That's all you've got for me?" he asked, his eyes finally back to their serpentine green. The fire no longer leaked from his nose, ears, and mouth. But the tremble of his frame had yet to evacuate.

"I can't say I'll be perfect," I started, dragging a palm down my face. "But I want to fix this." I moved my hand between us, trying not to break down. "I want to earn you too."

"You don't have to earn me, pet," he rasped, his broken tone matching my own. "Only promise to learn to love me back."

"Back?" I whispered, my voice dropping several octaves. I think I loved him the moment I set eyes on him. His commanding nature both scared and invited me in.

"Yes, back. Because the moment you fell to your knees and offered me your freedom, I was yours. I love you, your petulance and subservience. I love the anger and sass. I love the kisses and every touch you offer me. I love your sighs and all the fucking moans you give. But most of all, I love your fight, your passion, and the love you pretended didn't always exist right here."

He traced my tender skin once more, his eyes glowing, but this time differently. There was something freeing about his admission.

His hand anchored to my hair, gripping it and pulling me back. Lips met my flesh, and a whimper did him in.

He wasted no time to lift me, grabbing his cuff. My anxiety drilled into me as he held it. But it didn't bring us to Vex's, it flashed to an unrecognizable place.

"Welcome home, Valentine."

MAEVE BLACK

CHAPTER TWENTY-ONE
PYRO

Skinny Love - Birdy

I could already tell he didn't believe me. His eyes flashed with worry for only the briefest of moments before it shifted to awe.

The moment I left Arson's new place, I knew something that always kept me stable was the acknowledgement that putting my roots down mattered.

Sure, I had no inclination toward having children yet, but that didn't mean it wouldn't happen someday if Val and I chose it. Or if the Fates decided to fuck us both and put me in a melt.

The thought didn't freak me out, but we also had a lot to do before that point. Growing, adapting, and learning each other mattered the most.

We deserved time and patience, to nurture the love we built and foster a place between us where no worries or doubt existed.

His palm cupped my jaw. He offered no words as his eyes danced around the room. It was soft in here, darker and warm. The walls were soft browns, the wood-slatted wall only further bringing them together.

"What is this place?"

"Ours," I answered quickly. His attention dashed over the room, unable to stick to one place. The way he fit here made sense.

Dropping his hand, desperation took him to the kitchen. The countertops were stone, and while I didn't know if he liked cooking, I did. I put a little of us both in here. Gave him a permanent place where he couldn't doubt my commitment.

"It's beautiful." He turned away from me and I knew it was to hide whatever he was feeling. I walked over to him, not too quick as to frighten him. He was like a scared animal, wounded, learning to trust.

Tapping his shoulder, I waited for him to give me an in. Tentatively, his fingers reached for mine and I gripped them, twining our fingers.

"I'm not going anywhere," I reassured him, allowing him the space to choose his next move. He breathed heavily, a shudder racking his frame before he turned into me, wrapping his arms around my middle.

His face found its way onto my chest, nearly in the crook of my neck. "I want this." The words came out like a prayer and a promise all in one.

His honesty was all I ever wanted; his truth, and freedom. Right now, it felt that way. Like he truly trusted me with it.

I held him, wrapping both my arms and wings around his body. The softness in which he cried had me wanting to cocoon him in love and adoration. To protect him and hurt anyone who ever dared fuck with him.

"I love you, Pyro."

My chest throbbed with a new ache. Once, I could've said Val held my heart in his hands with hatred tearing it in half. But now, as he whispered the four words I wanted to hear more than anything, it was just a protective reaction that he held my heart with such sharp care.

His nails bit into me as he used them as a coping mechanism, squeezing and releasing them with each cry.

"I love you too, pet."

I kissed his forehead, his temple, his cheeks. Making my way to his nose, I playfully nipped at it, chastely kissing it after. Then his jaw, leading back to his mouth.

When our lips met this time, there was no anger, no hate, and definitely no resistance. This kiss was liberation, absolution, and he was mine.

Our hearts beat together, reaching for one another's in our chests. His tongue teased mine, flicking over my bottom lip, prodding, waiting.

I opened for him, allowing him all the exploration he wanted. He tasted of freedom, someone who finally could feel and express all he wanted.

He groaned when I teased back, flicking his tongue with the passion welling inside me. This wasn't even sexual, yet somehow my body didn't get the memo.

His hands dragged up my back, his rings digging into my flesh as he attempted to pull us closer together. There was no room left, not unless he somehow burrowed inside my veins like the potent heat did.

I pressed him into the counter, boxing him in. I placed my hands on either side of him, breaking our embrace.

No words were shared as we stared at each other. It should be awkward, the lack of conversation, the silence, but it didn't bother us.

Leaning forward, my lips traced his pulse point, feeling the blood hum as it tapped against me. I licked upward, wanting to taste the flavor of love. Because that was how his heart beat, with love.

Dragging my teeth downward, I nicked him with my fangs. No blood seeped out, but a stripe of red was there, begging for more.

"Pyro," he hummed, his hands still fisted in my shirt. "Make me yours."

A rumble rose from the depths of me, pleasing the monster beneath my skin. It growled with acknowledgement and as the noise left my throat, Val's fingers dug deeper into my back. My teeth elongated, and he didn't even flinch.

I didn't hold back, pressing my teeth into his neck. Euphoria met heat as I sunk inside his flesh. He whimpered, and his arousal filled my senses. He tasted warm like strawberries—and mine. Leaning into me, I held on to him.

It wasn't even the need to drink or absorb, it was the comfort of being connected. Blood dripped down his neck, the droplets wasted as I stayed hooked inside him. I could feel his hopes and his fears, taste his dreams and desires, and my cock pressed against my slacks forcefully, knowing what else this bond required.

"Please," he begged.

He didn't have to say more, I hummed with my release of his neck. Licking his bite, a feral need infused itself in my bones.

Our eyes connected, his traveling to the blood smattered on my lips, chin, and down my jaw. He leaned forward, his tongue darting out before he licked a long stripe up my throat. When he reached my lips, he pushed inside. Tasting himself and the heat of my desire.

"You have to bite me back," I rumbled around the words, almost promising him our downfall. With his return mark on me, we'd feel each other. And not just when our skin connected, but when we were away from each other.

If we felt anything, whether love, fear, happiness, or pain, we shared it. "Will it hurt?"

"I fucking hope so," I admitted, wanting the pain of his bite. He wasn't a dragon, his teeth weren't naturally sharp like mine. That didn't stop him from kissing me, his lips trailing down my throat. He didn't stop there, slipping from where I had him pinned.

His fingers went to my trousers, fumbling for only a moment as he released them. I thought it was cute, how he wanted to go for somewhere not visible.

"Is this okay?" he hesitantly asked, lifting the band of my boxer briefs. I nodded quickly and he pulled them down, my cock bobbing free. He glanced at it, licking his lips, but continued with what he wanted.

"Anywhere you want, baby," I rasped, heady lust filling me with all the possibilities.

"I want it right here," he admitted, tapping the thickest part of my thigh. He traced the spot reverently, his eyes blowing out with a mixture of lust and promise. "This way no one can see it but me."

The way the words escaped sounded animalistic, like his brand was only for his eyes. "Then do it," I coaxed, running my fingers through his hair. He leaned into my touch, then distracted me by tracing his tongue along my skin. Without guidance, his mouth sucked on my flesh before the drag of his teeth nearly had me buckling. His one hand held my ass, anchoring me to him, the other cupped the juncture of my thighs.

"That's it," I groaned around the arousal fueling my every breath. "Bite me."

His teeth dug into me, the pain making my cock throb. There was a part of me that wanted to stop him, to fuck him raw against the floor, but I let him continue.

They dug deeper, the pinch tight and hot. When he put more pressure, I felt the bruising start. It turned me on as much as the imprints of his rings did.

After a moment of him scarcely biting, I felt the stab of his teeth. Almost as if they somehow naturally grew. He sucked at my thigh, moaning. His face flushed as he continued to bite. He suckled, like he wanted and couldn't get enough of my taste.

Blood sharing was intimate for dragons, a bond no one could break. It meant forever. A vow weaved with magic.

We didn't need blood for sustenance, but seeing how Val seemed aroused at the consumption of mine had me wondering if it was something we'd have to try later.

When he pulled back, his lips were swollen, covered with blood, and the dazed expression did unspeakable things to me.

"I need to be inside you," I got out before lifting him up and heading down the hall. We skipped the rest of the impromptu house tour.

When we reached the room, I took no time to set him down and undress him. It wasn't hard, he only sported a simple tee, his boots, and jeans.

"I feel high," Val commented with a cough that turned into a chuckle. It was warm and unsurprising. Blood sharing came as an aphrodisiac affect. His fingers touched my button-up, and without preamble, he tugged it roughly, all the buttons flying away. "My bad."

The way his lips curved mischievously told me he wasn't sorry at all. With a growl, I lifted him onto the bed. His thighs split automatically, and I paused to relish in the fact that this man was mine.

His blood-covered neck brought me so much satisfaction, and I knew he felt the same about my thigh because his eyes strayed to it over and over.

I pushed his legs up, my body overheating. Reaching for the lube I knew was in the nightstand, excitement fueled me.

I was losing myself to my monster, and I didn't mind. He was relentless. With a pop of the cap, the lube bubbled out of the top. Pressing Val's legs to his chest, I squeezed the bottle, dripping it all over.

There was no hesitation or working him over for hours while he cried out. Time wasn't an issue anymore, and patience was nonexistent when he peered at me with as much adoration as possible.

Pressing one finger into him, he bore down. His eyes glazing over as I moved deeper. "Look at you taking me," I praised, leaning in to kiss his thigh. "Drives me insane when you clench."

"I need more," he panted, wiggling to use my finger for his pleasure. I added a second finger, my body begging to just sink into him and take what was mine.

"What, are you desperate for my cock?"

His eyes darkened and he nodded. "Please, Pyro. I need it."

I tsked, digging my thumb into his thigh. Red-hot lust shot straight to my balls when I scissored inside him. He moaned, exposing his marked throat.

That movement made me lose it, and I took my fingers out, coating my cock in lube and pressing home. He groaned as I bottomed out, and I hissed little pants as pleasure overtook every brain cell.

My fingers danced across his thigh, lifting it higher. "Look at me while I'm inside of you," I breathed out. His gaze snapped to mine with the command.

I'm so fucking gone for him.

LAUGH
BEST DAY
LOVE YOU
CARE 4 U
SWEET TALK
KISS ME
FRIEND ME
I ♥ YOU

CHAPTER TWENTY-TWO

VALENTINE

X - Nicky Jam, J Balvin

"*Look at me while I'm inside of you.*"

I didn't want to, the pleasure was too much to withstand. The intensity of which his eyes bore into mine wrecked me. He held my chin, his fingers digging into my face so there wasn't an escape. My throat throbbed from his teeth, but I swear I thought I'd blow my load in those moments. He latched onto me, staying there like that night at the club, just waiting out.

"Look at me, baby," he nearly begged, his voice gravelly and so fucking intense.

He knew intimacy scared me, but I also promised him I wouldn't run. Closing my eyes for the briefest of moments, I allowed myself to experience this.

To experience him.

We met somewhere in the center of ecstasy and starvation. The greens of his eyes nearly depleted by the black. His lips and mouth still red from biting me, but he never looked more appealing than at this very moment.

His hips smacked as he fucked into me with abandon. My balls ached with how badly I needed this. His hand that dug into my leg aggressively slid down my thigh, working my length in the next second.

He pumped me with purpose, making sure to press against my piercings, knowing it drove me near madness.

His grunts filled the room while he arched into me, doing all the work. Sharp pain pinched me as his wings dragged up and down my chest. His teeth dug into his lip, the look of pure determination mixing with pleasure etched between his eyebrows as his gaze devoured mine.

"This is what you do to me. You fucking wreck me, Valentine." His fist held tighter, moving in the sharp tempo of his thrusts. "I mean, look at you. You're fucking beautiful. Taking my cock so nicely."

He shifted my hips, prostrating them so he consistently pressed against that place inside me that ached for him.

"I could stay lost in you forever, fucking you every single day. You'd like that, wouldn't you?" *I would.*

I offered a nod, and he rewarded me with several strokes, knowing how to drive me mad. My body felt twisted, a knot tied over and over, creating a mess to never be undone. I reached out and touched his wings, and he let me. The moan that was ripped from him had me doing it again.

"Tell me you love me," he demanded, and as my eyes were caught in the heated flames of his, I knew he needed to hear it again.

"I love you," I gasped out as his grip tightened on me. He leaned forward, drooling over my tip, coating me in his heat.

His body came down, pressing my knee to my shoulder, bottoming out so we were flush together. "Again."

"I love you." A grunt wheezed out of him when I clenched down, needing to see him fall apart. "I fucking love you."

My words came out as cries as tears filled my eyes. Who knew admitting my feelings would feel so rewarding. There were so many emotions passing across his face, adoration, lust, but deeper than that, his eyes gave me understanding, a tenderness that made my body ache.

He let go of my cock, just soaking inside me, enjoying the clench of me around him. He nipped at my nipple, flicking his tongue over the metal. That didn't stop with one torturous stroke. He kept at it, acting as if it were ice cream, needing to get every last drop.

My body shook, the irritation of Pyro's actions both infuriating and maddening. It felt so good and bad together. A little flame puffed out of his mouth, and I lost it, bucking into the air, wild with the need of friction.

The heat danced across my skin as he continued to tease me. Just little flickers, enough to bring a touch of pain and then the arousal that diffused it.

"Touch yourself," he rasped, guiding me. My fingers wrapped around my shaft, the jolted zing of pleasure catching me off guard. "That's right." His eyes flicked between my subtle hand movements and my eyes, not sticking to one too long. "Harder." I squeezed, my eyes rolling back as the beat of my heart throbbed in the tip of my dick. "Brush your thumb over the piercings." His words were purely volcanic, hot and too irresistible.

"Pyro," I whimpered.

"Want to come, baby?" he rasped, his forehead wrinkled with his own strain.

I frantically nodded in response as he pulled back and pumped into me. It was aggressive and sharp, not soft or gentle. "Wait for me." He teased and tortured, punctuating his intentions. "I want to feel your release while I'm buried deep inside you."

"It feels too good," I hissed. "I'm not going to make it."

He gripped me with his hand once more, leaning forward. The moment his teeth sunk back into my throat, hot spurts of my release sprayed us both and I convulsed around him.

His movements didn't slow as he pounded into me. "That's good, so good," he groaned, his thrusts becoming jerky as he came inside me.

"I love you," I said once more, my body growing heavy with each breath.

"I love you too, Cupid."

MAEVE BLACK

EPILOGUE
PYRO

I Will Follow You Into The Dark - Death Cab for Cutie

"**P**lease don't make me."

I chuckled, unable to help myself. The pout on my husband's face was far too comical. We went to the human realm to go to a festival during Valentine's Day. They called it Crush.

Each year, they held it in a field. Massive. With DJs, live singers, and Valentine's-themed games.

I stared at the ring on his finger, the one that didn't match the rest. The one that labeled him as mine.

"Sorry, pet. You're going and we're making new traditions."

"You know I loathe Valentine's."

Kissing his jaw, I ignored that. "You don't hate them anymore, starting this year." He let out the lowest grumble.

I nipped his ear, scraping my teeth along his throat next. Even three years later, my mate mark on him had never looked better. "If you go, I'll let you suck me off."

His eyes darkened and his pout suddenly disappeared. "Okay, what are you waiting for? Let's go."

He was easy to please. Most days, I hated him blowing me. Not because he wasn't good at it. Quite the opposite. It was because he was so good at it that he had me squirting in minutes.

"Settle down, you're not even dressed the part."

"Absolutely the fuck not," he immediately argued, his face flushing. "You're not getting me in any Cupid garb. I don't care if it turns you on."

We both laughed at his concern because a deal was a deal. "Uh-uh," I tutted. "You going requires you to wear something that fits the theme."

"Fuck off," he grumbled. My hand trailed down my naked torso, settling over the clasp on my pants. "That's not fair at all." His eyes hadn't left my crotch, and I knew I had him right where I wanted.

"Come on, be a good boy and put this on. I even made sure it was black." His gazed flashed to mine with a tiny bit of hope.

Sure, it was black, but it was heavily Cupid themed. I handed him the bag, and his hesitance before grabbing it made me laugh.

"If I do this, you have to let me dress you?"

My mind wandered to what he could possibly make me wear that would bother me. And that was nothing.

"Fine, but be quick about it."

He practically ran to our bedroom. When I heard a loud "*What the fuck!*" I couldn't resist my snort. After about five minutes, a grumbling Valentine came back. And fuck, if we didn't leave, I'd be taking him right here and now.

"No," he complained, noting my arousal. "You're not allowed to get off on this."

The outfit I bought him went perfectly with his normal attire. It was black and leather. A big heart sat at the center of his chest. It was connected and strapped across his shoulders, his abs, and in the back clasped with a lock.

Adorned with studs, he looked delicious.

His jeans were similar to what he usually wore, except this one was attached to the harness I bought him. But what I was sure actually got him, the thing that made it so Cupid-like, was the fact that emblazoned on that center heart was the words *Kiss Me, I'm Cupid*.

It was perfect and he looked like a snack as I admired him. "Okay, lay it on me. What are you making me wear?"

As if he'd been planning it his whole life, he raised his pierced eyebrow, smirking. "It's on the bed."

Shit.

The smugness he exhibited told me I should be worried.

I walked to our room in trepidation, the wood floor making little noises as if it wanted to detail every movement I made.

When I entered, the room was covered in red balloons.

On the ceiling, the floor, and even across our bed were all things red. Rose petals decorated everything too. And in the center of the bed sat a big, comically huge box that looked identical to a conversation heart one.

Before I could go over to it, hands wrapped around me from behind. "I haven't hated Valentine's Day since you bought me a heart of chocolates."

He held me, kissing my neck, my shoulders, and then biting into me as he admired my body. I turned to him, his eyes blazing with arousal.

"Happy Valentine's Day, my love. Now, open that box."

I picked up the massive box while he held on to me, nuzzling his face in my neck. It felt light, but with a little shake, the sound of something clattering hit my ears.

Opening the top, I turned it upside down. There were three hearts, and once rearranged, they said.

Immediately, I turned toward him. Our gazes locked, and a mischievous expression danced over his face.

"What—"

He put a finger to my lips, reaching beneath our bed to grab another box. Like the black one that haunted my dreams, one that matched was in his hands.

Placing the box in front of me, he made an open it gesture, raising his eyebrows in expectation. I only had to grasp it for it to unwind itself.

Anxiety lived freely through me as it unraveled and popped open. My heart hadn't stopped its odd rhythm as I waited for whatever Valentine planned.

Taking a deep breath, I braced myself for whatever came next. In my hands was a folded suit. It was similar to my usual tailored ones, except this one was red.

On top was a white letter. Setting down the suit, I opened it. When the scent of Christmas hit my nose, I knew immediately who it was from.

BROTHER,

FORGIVE ME FOR TAKING SO LONG. I KNOW IT'S SEVEN YEARS EARLY, AND IF NOT FOR VALENTINE'S PERSISTENCE AND JOYFUL'S HEART, I WOULDN'T HAVE PIECED IT TOGETHER.
I DIDN'T NEED THE RED SUIT TO ACKNOWLEDGE WHAT IT MEANT TO BE SANTA. HELL, I DIDN'T EVEN NEED ANYONE—ESPECIALLY NOT XÓ—TO REMIND ME WHAT CHRISTMAS SPIRIT WAS.
YOU WERE THERE ALL ALONG.
SO, THIS IS YOUR FIRST, BROTHER.

P.S. YOU'RE STILL AN UPTIGHT ASS, BUT I GUESS IT MAKES SENSE.

ARSON

"My first what?" I asked, humor and awe lacing my tone. At some point, Valentine must've moved, because now he sat on a chair, leaning back, mirroring my pose from Vex's.

He still wore his hot-as-hell Cupid getup, but on his head adorned a Santa hat. This one was black with white trimming.

His hand snaked down his chest, tugging on the straps seductively. He ascended to his thighs, and like the cocky little shit he was, he tapped his thigh.

"Sit."

"Oh, really?" I asked, raising my eyebrows. He nodded, no amusement on his face, trying his hardest to appear like me.

I walked over to him, his eyes not once leaving mine. He commanded my every step and a part of me loved being at his mercy.

Unlike the brat beneath me, I sat without complaint. "Are you going to tell me what he meant by 'first'?"

Val shushed me with another finger and I couldn't help but nip at it. He broke character then, his lips curving with amusement.

"What would you like for Christmas, Pyro. I know you've been such a good boy."

My face morphed with the sarcasm in his eyes. I was far from a good boy, but I played into his little game.

"You, naked. Tied up, preferably. Where I force orgasm after—" He quieted me again, this time with his mouth, a perfect distraction.

"Okay, this is not going to work." He stood, bringing me with him, his jeans strained with his erection.

"You take the lead."

We switched and I sat down. My dick twitched as he lowered onto me without being asked. He turned toward me, his hand fisting my hair. "Ask me."

I swallowed the dryness of my throat, not knowing where he intended to go with this. "What do you want for Christmas, pet?" It came out strained, my cock pressing against my slacks as his skin pressed against my bare chest.

He leaned forward, licking a path from my Adam's apple to my ear. "I want you to be Santa."

Turning our faces toward each other, our lips accidentally brushed, the metal of his piercings tickling my lip.

"I-I can't," I answered, realizing I wasn't Santa. I could dress like him, even know the ins and outs of the job, but I wasn't him.

"That's what he meant. This is your first. Your first Christmas as the Jolly Boy."

"How?"

"Xó and I spoke every day for the last year, planning, scheming, and we both made Arson realize that he clung onto being Santa because he felt he had to make up for a lot."

"What if I suck at it?"

Val immediately shook his head, his eyebrows scrunched together with determination. "You're the perfect man for the job. You've lived your entire life for this moment."

He kissed me then as realization set in. My husband, the man I've given my heart and soul to, did the unaskable. Something I could never wish for, and made it my reality.

"I love you," I whispered.

"I know."

His eyes met mine, and everything in me wanted to make him feel good forever. To make him happy and be everything he needed.

Without a word, I lifted him with me, tossing him on the bed. He let out a little grunt as I tore his pants down his legs. Underneath, he wore nothing. Bare. Just for me.

Tapping his legs, my words came out harsh. "Spread."

He didn't argue, but split his legs, his body pliant for me. Gripping both of his cheeks, I parted them and dove in. My tongue pressed against the rough flesh, licking and biting over every part I could reach. I was feverish and so beyond turned on. I just needed him to feel as good as I did.

"Fuck, Pyro," he let out, his body shuddering as I speared inside him. His ass pressed into my face, fucking himself on my tongue.

Replacing my tongue with my fingers, I slid inside him, wasting no time to prep him. He whined as I stretched him, needing to be inside.

Once he shook from the pleasure, begging me to fuck him, I stood. Pulling off my pants and boxer briefs, I laid on the bed, my cock nearly saluting.

"I want you to ride me, baby. Take your pleasure. Please."

I wasn't a beggar, and I sure as hell didn't usually lay pliant. But this time, I wanted him fucking me from on top. There was an unspoken desire to have him take whatever pleased him because he was so good for me. He deserved a reward.

"Spread your wings," he commanded softly, but the heat in his eyes did me in. Whenever Val got his hands on my wings, I came every time. It was part of the reason I forced his hands away when we fucked. If he knew the control he had just by grazing his fingers across me, he'd torture me like I did him.

I unfurled them, spreading my wings out, and he took no time climbing over me. The bed dipped as he settled on top of me, his harness being all that was left.

His fingers tiptoed across my wings, gentle but firm. Pleasure shot straight to my balls as he teased the skin, but he kept to his torturous pace.

I groaned, unable to stop the pulsing between my thighs. Val leaned over me, nipping at my nipple before kissing the soft flesh of my wings.

"You're going to be the death of me," I rumbled, and as a result, he bit the flesh and I bowed into him. "You goddamn tease."

He chuckled, licking across the cartilage, making sure to suck every time my body started to relax. His teasing alone could make me come, and I was sure that was his intent.

My cock leaked all across my stomach as he grinded on me. This was his game of torture, and I was the conduit of all the energy.

"When I lick your wings, I feel like I'm sucking you off," he mused aloud, punctuating his statement with a long stripe across the most sensitive part of my wings.

"Feels that way," I groaned.

"Let's find out." The way in which his words taunted me wasn't lost on either of us. He lowered himself above my cock and took my entire length in his mouth, not stopping when he gagged and not letting up even when I gripped his hair.

His tongue piercings were one of evil creation. He pressed them against the massive vein on the underside of my dick, and when he swallowed me down, they wrecked me.

"You're too fucking good at this," I rasped. "No one takes cock like you." He moaned around me and my balls pulsed with the vibrations. After a few more near-orgasm-inducing sucks, he popped off with a smile.

Taking no time to catch his breath or to let me calm the fuck down, he reached over to our nightstand and grabbed a bottle of lube.

Pouring the sticky liquid over my cock, he spread it all the way to my base. With zero extra prep, he hovered over me and slammed down.

"Valentine," I growled, grasping him in a death grip while my body went through shock waves. My release was at the cusp and as he flattened his palms on my wings, scratching his nails down them, I roared.

VALENTINE

"Slow down," he demanded underneath me. I'd never felt more powerful than now with his cock buried deep inside me and my hands all over his sensitive flesh.

He knew how aware I was when it came to his wings. I loved watching him fall apart by my doing.

I didn't slow down, I rode him harder and faster, whimpering along the way. "Are you overwhelmed?" I asked him, my voice husky. He growled at me in response. "Good, because you're going to make me come."

He groaned as I bounced higher, causing him to almost leave my body before slamming down. "You were made to fuck me," I said on a breathy exhale. "It's so hard to focus when you make those noises."

His roar was my only warning before he flipped me onto my knees and plowed into me. The thrusts were manic, messy, and they hit every mark. When his hand came down on my ass, hard and unrelenting, I swore stars flashed before my eyes. I cried as he hit him again and again. The pain bled into pleasure and my cock ached at the lack of touch.

"Look at what you made me do," he hissed, punctuating his anger with both his hips and slaps to my ass. "You couldn't help yourself, could you? Wanting to be good but ending up being bad."

I whined as my dick leaked, leaving streaks on the bed as I humped it for friction. "Are you overwhelmed, baby?" I nodded, reaching to stroke myself. "Good, you've earned it."

"Please make me come," I all but begged him. His thrusts became slower and he reached around to grasp me in his hand.

"Do you hear yourself, baby? How you're a whimpering mess begging for me to make you come? I want to hear you call my name as I fuck you. And when you're coming, I want you to squeeze me." I'd do anything for my orgasm, so I nodded frantically. He fisted me, his strokes rough and quick, matching his unrelenting pace.

"I'm going to come," I warned him, feeling my balls tighten as he pumped continuously.

"You're such a good boy, Cupid. You can come for me. Squeeze my cock."

"Pyro, fuck," I hissed, his words doing me in. I pulsed, throbbing with each spurt of my orgasm. It just kept going and going and he didn't stop pressing inside me.

"You've made me feel so good," he grunted, his legs shaking from behind me. "You're so fucking perfect."

With a few more punching thrusts, he let out a roar, bringing me with him when he crashed onto the bed.

"I fucking love you," he raggedly admitted, stroking my arm.

"I know," I teased softly. "Happy Valentine's Day, Santa."

His entire face lit up with that, and I just knew, he'd be the best red suit man the world would ever see.

KEEP READING FOR A LITTLE BIT OF
DEAR MONSTER CLAUS.

CHAPTER 1

JINGLE BELL ROCK — BOBBY HELMS

XO

Another romance in the books, and once again, it's not mine.

The couple in question was two women. Fiona and Lena. When given their names on the *lucky-in-love* list, excitement filled me. They'd never met, the tension had my palms sweating with nerves. It can go so many ways, but theirs painted a softer and new picture. Two women who hid for so long and finally found each other in the end. As soon as I passed them both, I sent them silent love magic.

They'd get married, grow a life together, and create a little antique shop in town. One I'll be back to visit in a few years.

Now, I sit in the tiny coffee shop at the edge of Mistletoe Grove, drinking away my hopes and desires for my own future.

My sisters, Dulce and Dionysius, chat with other humans, pushing them toward their soul mates while I stand near Valentine. Unlike the three of us, he doesn't have a charge. He's just not too fond of being around our parents.

Instead, we drag him around with us during his downtime.

He's downing some Christmas concoction I convinced him to try, his face scrunched with displeasure. "How do you drink this shit?" I lift my mug, the reindeer with a red nose on the ceramic smiling back at me. I haven't tried this year's recipe, but last year's was hazelnut and toffee surprise.

Taking a sip, warmth fills my body. Flavors coat my tongue, tasting like holiday spirit. Cinnamon, chocolate, and a bit of clove. Steam rises from the cup, making little swirls as my brother dramatically rolls his eyes. His fingers tap on his backup cup of Earl Grey.

"It tastes like Christmas in a cup," I persist, smacking my lips to figure out the last flavor that evades me. *Maybe it's nutmeg?*

Val narrows his eyes at me and then my drink as if it offends him. His lips form around the edge of the cup as he tastes it once more.

"Christmas in a cup? More like I'm licking a pine tree in the dead of winter," he grumbles, gagging openly.

I laugh at his annoyance, patting his shoulder. He was never one for festivity or the cold. I nod toward our sisters, wondering how they commit to giving everyone love without questioning where our happy endings lie.

We could find love for any person in all the realms, yet we don't get it ourselves? Make it make sense. I've felt like such an outsider in my realm and family. I'm the only one hoping what only mortals wish for.

It's ridiculous, knowing that my people judge me for having ideas of happiness.

I want a man, but not any man. I want one who wants me and *only me*.

"Why don't we get to have love?" I gently whisper, hoping *he* didn't hear. It's a topic of contention between us. Hades, I even know his response—he gives it often. He's always telling me to stop being so obsessed with the idea of romance. It's not for *us*.

We have rules.

Drinking more, I eye him and note his wrung-out expression. His eyebrows draw inward, pinching while his lips purse, yet he says nothing. A tic in his jaw forms too, it's his usual bitter expression. A mix of disappointment and annoyance.

We're Cupids, the myths, or rather the reality. There isn't just one of us, it's a family business. We all play our parts, helping the world find their forever partners.

"Xóchitl," he sighs with exasperation. Val only uses my full name when he isn't happy. Usually, it's Xó or Xóchi. With a shake of his head, he pats my arm. "We're not meant to find what we give others. That's what makes us perfect for the job. We don't seek that kind of thing. We're not created to."

Yet, my yearning lingers, growing stronger with every passing match. Why not us? We don't even experience love through our charges. It's like we witness it, seeing it through their eyes, without ever knowing the feeling.

"Why though? Why can't I experience hugs, kisses, and possibly more?"

He cringes, almost like I'm reading my diary out loud. "That's just not in the cards for us."

Anger rises in me. None of my siblings seem to care, but every time I see someone fall in love, watch their eyes shine with hope and infatuation, I sadden further. I've never felt it, I've never experienced warmth in that way, I've never had sex, or even had an orgasm. I've never even *kissed* someone before.

My cheeks warm, thinking of how embarrassing it must be to others to know I'm as old as I am and have never experienced affection.

"I want to experience love," I solemnly admit, my voice quieting. Gripping my mug like it's a protectant, I wait for his reactionary response. It's still warm, but the cold bitterness inside me festers at the possibility that I'll never truly be happy. "I want to experience romance."

I can only talk to Val. Dion and Dulce make fun of my desire for simple things. They're twins and don't understand humanity or its need for emotions.

That's probably why they toy with them so much.

Val shakes his head again, his jaw clenched. He's probably sick of my wondrous questions, but until there's a definitive answer other than *just because,* I'll continue to question everything. My brother and I are closest. Not only in age, but in similarities. We have the same hobbies and joys. Except that he hates Christmas—and holidays altogether. Whereas I could live every single day as a holiday and never grow tired.

"Can't you distract yourself?" he grumpily wonders. "It's Christmas, you like Christmas. Maybe it'll get your mind off what's off-limits for us."

My lip protrudes as I acknowledge my true denial. I've helped thousands find love. Why is it so hard for me?

We're taught young; Cupids don't find love, they give it. They don't find contentment, they let others experience it. They don't get romance, they simply thrust it upon others.

I've never wanted to deny my heritage or family business more than now. I stare at the surrounding shops. The dangling lights, window-painted snowmen, and how there's a massive tree in the center of town, illuminating everything. Or it will be once Christmas week hits.

Mistletoe Grove is where we go every year. They gave each Cupid family an area. We're fortunate to go to the human realm, to a place where they celebrate holidays.

Back in Darchon, we don't have such celebrations. It's gloomy all year, wars are always on the cusp. But here exists joy, laughter, cookies, and love. Val stares at me, his eyes almost studying as I absorb the merriment of the town.

"Fine, but don't harass me when I end up staying here for the winter," I nonchalantly shrug, taking another drink, and decide that's what I'll do. There are no other love matches on my duties until New Year's. All I have is time.

Val offers a small smile. He doesn't like when I'm sad. Unlike him and our sisters, I'm the youngest. They say that's why I always crave forbidden things, but I wonder if they're just lost.

"If you stay too long, we'll have to come back and drag you home. Especially if you miss a check-in. We all know you hate writing letters." He says this with raised eyebrows and a spark of amusement. He may be jaded from the Cupid business, but he's always been an amazing brother.

"Thanks, Val." I push out my chair, reaching for him to hug. He gives me an awkward side one. Another thing we don't do. *Affection*. Cupids call hugs human behavior. He's wrong. Even when we're in Darchon, giving love magic to monsters and fae alike, we see them embrace.

"Now, go." He shoos me, his hands waving quickly. "Dion and Dulce won't like you going off."

"That's because they're boring workaholics with no hobbies," I mutter grumpily, thinking of how they always tease me for my fascinations. Humor lights his features, his dimples peeking through.

"They like teasing poor human boys," he argues, but he's very amused.

"That's not a hobby, Val," I grumble, thinking about how they can turn invisible and cause chaos. "That's called harassment."

I set down my nearly empty mug and grab my bag with our special letters that'll send directly to my home in Darchon. Cupids are magical, not like wizards or Wiccans, but definitely in their own right. We could create love, manipulate the weather, and induce happiness temporarily.

"See you after Christmas!" I call out, heading toward the door before he can argue. Sometimes, while Val tries his best, he still dampers my mood. He's moody and unhappy.

Now it's time to find love. No matter how asinine it sounds to everyone else. Val might think I'm celebrating Christmas—which I will—but my intentions are clear. I'll find my happy ending this December.

CHAPTER 2

A HOLLY JOLLY CHRISTMAS - BURL IVES

XO

Cold welcomes me back at the cabin. It sits at the opposite edge of town. Old, but furnished, and so stunning during the winter. I've been here for over a week, and already I'm settled in comfortably.

We've had this place for generations. A home to escape to if we're stuck in the snow for the winter. Mistletoe Grove gets blizzards that are insanely packed. Where you can't even make it to a portal and head home.

I need to go into town for snacks. Not because I need human food to sustain me, but because it's my guilty pleasure. Especially sweets. Candy canes, cookies, and gingerbread. My absolute weaknesses.

Pulling on my dress, I go for simple. An ugly green sweater dress with little reindeer on them. It's so contrasting against my skin that it'll possibly act as a distraction.

I'm a pink color, more like light bubble gum rather than bright pink.

All Cupids have different pigmentation. Val is redder in tone, while Dion is lavender and Dulce is a peach. I think it's the only way they tell us apart.

We're similar in the looks department, especially since Dion and Dulce are twins. Our noses match and our lips too. Our eyes all match our skin tones, unironically. If not for cosplayers in the human realm, our coloring would stand out more, be awkward even. We get comments, but using the 'oh, we're from a convention' has them moving along.

Unlike many faefolk from Darchon, we don't have any fun attributes other than our coloring. If dragons were still around, they'd have scales and wings. Of course, they can glamour those, but they generally showed them. Even many incubi have horns and tails, and then there are the *Saephyn*. They have *fangs!* They don't like being called vamps, though.

After putting on some makeup, I head for the mall in town. There's only one, plus many mom-and-pop shops that have gifts and more niche items.

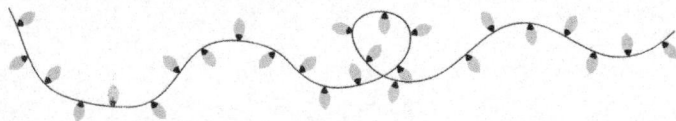

Once I arrive, I note all the Christmas lights twinkling. It's always so bright here, everyone's so nice and cheery. It's as if they save all the kindness for the month of December.

They decorated the inside with so many icicles, cut-out snowflakes, inflated snowmen, and even a Grinch holding a wreath mischievously. People mill about paying no mind to the beauty that is this place, but I stop at every shop to gawk.

Little kids giggle and one says, "Santa is here. He's granting wishes."

I'm not naïve, I've been told Santa is fictional. Something big businesses created to garner more money. But what if he's not? What if, like Cupids, he's very much *real*? I've watched movies, they're so cheerful and cute, and Santa always grants the good kids happiness. My heart races at the possibility, the acknowledgment that he could grant me my one wish.

Love.

Most people wish for money, success, or even something big. I just want to find love.

"Think he'll get me a guitar?" one kid asks, taking a bite out of a soft pretzel. Their face is full of excitement, something I feel reflected in me.

"Didn't you kick Mr. Daniel's a couple months ago?" another child asks with a raised eyebrow. They drink something and silently judge their friend.

"Yeah, but I apologized!" the first kid shouts, their face wobbling with worry. I know that if I made a single mistake and lost all chances at love, I'd be near tears too.

"Don't be mean, Rach. Johnny didn't mean it. Santa is forgiving," one parries, wrapping their arm around the one they called Johnny. I want to hug them both, tell them their hearts are big and compassion is such a wonderful trait, but I don't. Instead, they trail off and I look for this Santa fellow.

While meandering, the scent of cinnamon and cardamom distracts me. My nose drags me to a little shop, filled with nuts, roasted and coated ones specifically. A petite older person in a dress stands at the counter, cheeks red and sporting the cutest gray curls.

"Hello, dear," they offer, their voice cheery and kind.

"It smells delicious," I muse, taking in a deep breath and laughing when the person scrunches their face in amusement.

"They're quite tasty. I definitely recommend the pecans," they suggest, walking toward a tower of bags. The cellophane is decorated with tiny trees and stars. "It's the perfect mixture of sweet and salty."

"I'll take one!" My mind fills with the desire to munch them all down. The clerk ties off a bag with some frilly metallic material and heads to the register. I realize there's a chance that they know where Santa is. "Do you know where Santa is?" I shyly ask, not wanting to get a weird look from the person.

"Oh, yes! He's in the center of the mall. You won't miss the North Pole. There are lights and a Candy Cane Lane." They pause, smiling widely. "There are reindeer and a huge throne, too."

"How does one ask for a wish?" I awkwardly ask, hope sliding through me like the best tasting hot cocoa.

"You sit on his lap and ask for what you want. Be specific and try to ask for only one thing," they offer with a nod. Handing over my nuts, they point toward what I'm guessing is the center of the mall. "Head that way. You can't miss it. And if he doesn't respond the way you want, you can always mail Santa a letter. Those, he always reads thoroughly."

"Thank you so much!" The way hope soaks me with happiness has me skipping in the direction they told me to go.

MAEVE BLACK

MONSTERS, FAE, SMUT
& MORE SMUT

MEET MAEVE

Maeve Black writes fantasy, paranormal, and monster romance that they've always wanted to read. As someone who is queer, fat, and Latine, Maeve tries to be diverse and inclusive with all works, helping others see that the world isn't just a social construct. They love reading, playing fantasy video games, and drawing in their spare time. Maeve wants to be known for their spice and unique takes on the monsters they choose to write.

Printed in Great Britain
by Amazon